H...

romance
by Anne Mather
comes to life
on the movie screen

starring

KEIR DULLEA · SUSAN PENHALIGON

Leopard in the Snow

Guest Stars
KENNETH MORE · BILLIE WHITELAW

featuring GORDON THOMSON as MICHAEL
and JEREMY KEMP as BOLT

Produced by JOHN QUESTED and CHRIS HARROP
Screenplay by ANNE MATHER and JILL HYEM
Directed by GERRY O'HARA
An Anglo-Canadian Co-Production

Other titles by
ANNE HAMPSON
IN HARLEQUIN ROMANCES

Other titles by
ANNE HAMPSON
IN HARLEQUIN PRESENTS

Many of these titles are available at your local bookseller
or through the Harlequin Reader Service.

For a free catalogue listing all available Harlequin Romances,
send your name and address to:

HARLEQUIN READER SERVICE,
M.P.O. Box 707, Niagara Falls, N.Y. 14302
Canadian address: Stratford, Ontario, Canada N5A 6W2

or use order coupon at back of book.

Fly Beyond the Sunset

by

ANNE HAMPSON

Harlequin Books

TORONTO • LONDON • NEW YORK • AMSTERDAM • SYDNEY

Original hardcover edition published in 1977
by Mills & Boon Limited

ISBN 0-373-02163-1

Harlequin edition published May 1978

Copyright © 1977 by Anne Hampson. All rights reserved.

Except for use in any review, the reproduction or utilization of this
work in whole or in part by any form by any electronic, mechanical
or other means, now known or hereafter invented, including xero-
graphy, photocopying and recording, or in any information storage or
retrieval system, is forbidden without the permission of the publisher.
All the characters in this book have no existence outside the imagination of the author and have no relation whatsoever to anyone bearing
the same name or names. They are not even distantly inspired by
any individual known or unknown to the author, and all the incidents
are pure invention.

The Harlequin trademark, consisting of the word HARLEQUIN and the
portrayal of a Harlequin, is registered in the United States Patent
Office and in the Canada Trade Marks Office.

Printed in U.S.A.

CHAPTER ONE

MRS SHERIDAN stood in the doorway of the pink and cream bedroom and gazed anxiously at her daughter.

'I do wish you weren't so optimistic about this job, darling. I'm so afraid you're in for a bitter disappointment.'

Faun turned, swivelling round on the pretty, velvet-covered stool, a silver-backed hairbrush in her hand.

'I've managed to get an interview,' she reminded her mother with a smile, 'which is more than you thought I would when I sent in my application form.'

'In my opinion it was sheer chance.'

'Chance? How can you say that?'

'Whoever granted you the interview most probably believed you to be a man.'

'Why should he?'

'You told me yourself that you signed both the form and the accompanying letter Rendall F. Sheridan, deliberately omitting the name by which you're known—Faun. But in any case, as there are so few females with the particular qualifications required by the firm, they'd naturally take it for granted that no woman could apply for the post.' Mrs Sheridan wagged a forefinger in a gesture of warning. 'They won't want a girl, you mark my words!'

'I'm not a girl; I'm twenty-six.'

'Darling, you look a mere child! Take a glance at yourself in the mirror, then estimate your chances of competing with the male applicants.'

Swivelling around again, Faun thoughtfully examined the face that looked back at her. She had to admit that her appearance was deceptive and therefore it might go against her. True, there was strength in the beautiful lines and contours of her face, and there was a special steadfastness in the large, widely-spaced blue-grey eyes and even something unusually firm in the little pointed chin. But the long, glowing chestnut hair, the flawless transparency of her skin, through which could be discerned the blue veins at her temples, the full compassionate mouth ... all these compounded to take at least five years off her age.

'Perhaps you're right,' she conceded, though not one small degree of her optimism was lost in this admission. Female airline pilots were rare, but by no means unknown, and she herself had a great deal to offer. She spoke French and German fluently; she had the necessary flying experience, was in possession of excellent testimonials from her employers, Northern Territory Aviation of Australia, and from the air training school at Hamble where she had received the instruction which led to her gaining her Civil Pilot's and Navigator's certificates. She could handle an aeroplane as expertly as any pilot she knew, so to her logical way of thinking, it was reasonable to assume that her chance of obtaining the post was equal to that of any other applicant.

'I know I'm right,' her mother was saying. 'Do give up the idea, Faun. Phone this man—this personnel manager—and tell him you've changed your mind.'

'What a defeatist attitude, Mother!' Faun gave a little laugh of amusement, staring at her mother through the mirror. 'I've absolutely nothing to lose. In fact, I'm tremendously optimistic about my chances of landing this job.'

'They'll choose a man before you,' returned Mrs Sheridan emphatically.

'What about the Sex Discrimination Act?' challenged Faun, beginning to brush her hair.

'Oh, that!' scoffed her mother as if it didn't mean a thing. 'They'll get round it somehow.'

'They can't get round it. It's the law.'

Mrs Sheridan gave a deep sigh and fell silent for a space. Faun continued to stare at her through the mirror, noting the lovely slender figure with its alluring curves. An up-and-coming ballet dancer in her youth —before she gave up all for marriage—Mrs Sheridan still managed to retain the exquisite form which nature had bestowed upon her, an inheritance she had passed on to both her daughters.

'Well, if you really are determined,' she said at last, glancing at the clock on Faun's dressing-table, 'you'd better be moving. You did say the appointment was for half-past eleven?'

'That's right.' Faun also glanced at the clock. 'I've plenty of time.'

The waiting-room which she entered an hour later was, to say the least, impressive, with its deep-pile carpet of purple, its damask wall coverings and expensive lounge chairs upholstered in lilac moquette. On one wall there was hung a huge oil painting of one of the luxurious air limousines used by the firm, whose business it was to provide an entirely trouble-free air taxi service between Britain and the Continent. Owned by millionaire Clive Tarrant, the firm was used by wealthy businessmen, film stars and other important people. Its name was famous and from the moment she had read the advertisement in *The Times*, Faun had set her heart on becoming one of its pilots.

Taking possession of a chair, Faun leant back, completely relaxed and ready for the interview. Soon after her arrival a man entered, a man with the unmistakable stamp of an R.A.F. pilot. After staring at Faun for a moment he took up one of the magazines lying on the table and began to flick through the pages. Faun smiled to herself; the man had concluded that she had nothing at all to do with the advertisement for a co-pilot with this most exclusive of air taxi firms.

Both he and Faun glanced up as the door to an inner office swung open and a tall man emerged. Another applicant, decided Faun, scanning his face in an attempt to gain something from his expression. He had had his interview, and appeared to be a trifle flustered. The young lady who accompanied him to the door looked askance at Faun as she rose from her chair, preparing to enter the office. With a slight shrug of her shoulders the girl stood aside for Faun to pass in front of her; then she closed the door and disappeared through another at the other side of the office. The man left behind in the waiting-room had cast a most surprised glance at Faun, but that was nothing to the look of blank amazement which leapt to the face of the man in the office—Mr Greenway, who was to interview her.

'Are you Rendall Sheridan?' he inquired frowningly. Faun said yes, then went on to explain that although

Rendall was her first name, she was known as Faun.

'I'm afraid that Rendall is one of those family names which are so often inflicted on poor helpless infants.' She laughed, though, as she had never resented having been given her father's name. He was a pilot and he it was who had fired her with the desire to fly aeroplanes.

Whatever Mr Greenway thought of her unusual name was not to be read from his expression, nor did his voice reveal anything as he invited her to sit down.

Calm and composed, Faun accepted the chair indicated and, slowly removing her gloves, she placed them on her lap.

The man opposite was staring at her, clearly at a loss as to his choice of words.

'I must admit, at once,' he began eventually, 'that I hadn't expected a young lady to apply for the job.'

'No,' murmured Faun, certain that he had known that Rendall F. Sheridan was a female then he would have refused her the interview. However, an optimist at heart, she felt confident of landing the post once this man had learned of her accomplishments and experience. He knew her age, as she had inserted it in the space provided on the application form, yet he said, slowly and curiously,

'Might I inquire your age, Miss Sheridan?'

She told him, saw that he registered both surprise and regret.

'I'm very capable in spite of my appearance,' she added swiftly, not at all caring for that sign of regret in his eyes. 'I have all the qualifications asked for, and the experience. And, Mr Greenway, I have much more besides.' Faun hesitated about continuing, seeing that the

9

man was still a little unsure of whether or not to terminate the interview at once. However, it was soon clear to her—with her quick intelligence and woman's intuition —that Mr Greenway was exceedingly intrigued by his applicant, so he would at least give her a hearing. This he did, and for the next fifteen minutes or so he continued to put questions to her, listening with almost rapt attention to her answers and explanations. He then said, as if to himself,

'A pilot's and navigator's licences ...' His eyes fell to her application form, lying on the desk in front of him. 'You obtained your Captain's Certificate with Northern Territory Aviation, I see.'

'That's right.'

'And for the last ten months you've been taking over their V.I.P. staff operations?'

Faun nodded her head, aware that the man's expression was now one of deep admiration, and she knew that this admiration was solely for her accomplishments.

'Yes, that's correct, Mr Greenway.'

He seemed to give an inward sigh, and to her surprise she saw a return of that hint of regret.

'You have your log book with you?'

'Yes.' She took it from the slim briefcase she had brought with her and passed it to him across the desk. She watched him peruse it closely, noting the widening of his eyes as the long list of her varied and important duties passed before his astonished and appreciative gaze. At last he glanced up, his eyes flickering over her face, a face that seemed so young and fragile now, as Faun waited anxiously for his comments.

'You must be exceedingly proud of this.' He tapped

the log book which he still held in his hand. 'I must say, it contains one of the most impressive lists of V.I.P.s I've ever seen.'

'I've carried a fair number of the world's important people,' she agreed with a sort of quiet modesty that yet was very naturally tinged with pride. Mr Greenway was obviously impressed by this modesty, since it showed on his face. 'You will also see,' added Faun, breaking the silence that had fallen, 'that I'm fully conversant with the type of aircraft you operate here.'

The man sitting on the other side of the desk nodded his head, but for the moment he said nothing, and Faun looked speculatively at him, noticing the greying hair, the rather drawn lines of his face which—she felt sure—made him appear much older than he was. His lips were colourless except for the slight bluish tinge coming through the rather parched skin. It struck her forcibly that Mr Greenway was not in the best of health.

He spoke at length, commenting belatedly on what she had said about being conversant with the type of aircraft used by this particular firm.

'Yes, you must be conversant with our aircraft, seeing that you've flown similar machines on so many occasions.'

'I've not only operated them with Northern Territory Aviation, but also during my pilot training at Hamble.'

Mr Greenway paused again.

'I haven't yet asked why you want to change your job.'

'I prefer to work with a private company.'

'I see. But at present you are working with a large,

11

world-famous company, Miss Sheridan.'

'I took this job to gain experience, but it's always been my ambition to fly for a private company.'

'Do your employers know that you have applied for this post?'

'Yes, of course. They don't want me to leave, but on the other hand they know of my desires. They'll release me at once if I'm successful in being given the post.' Becoming more and more optimistic with every moment that passed—as there was no mistaking the fact that she had made as good an impression as it was possible for any applicant to make—Faun was astounded when, on handing her back her log book, Mr Greenway said,

'Without doubt I'm extremely impressed by your capabilities with aircraft, Miss Sheridan, but unfortunately I am not in a position to offer you the job.'

A profound silence followed this unexpected statement.

'I don't understand, Mr Greenway,' said Faun, staring at him. He made no answer, merely shifting uneasily in his chair. 'If you knew you couldn't offer me the job then why have you wasted both your time and mine by asking all those questions?' Her voice carried a ring of sharpness, reflecting her rising anger and disappointment.

'My only excuse is that I was intrigued by the unusual. There are few women of your age who have so much to offer.' He looked apologetically at her. 'Do forgive me, Miss Sheridan.'

She glanced down, her lips trembling. Never in her life had she met with a disappointment as great as this.

'Do you mind telling me your reasons for turning me down?' she managed to inquire at length, lifting her head and hoping that her eyes were not as bright as she suspected they were. 'I consider that, after spending all this time here, answering your questions, I'm entitled to an explanation.'

He nodded in agreement, a frown between his eyes. It was plain that he was feeling far from comfortable.

'You're obviously not aware, Miss Sheridan, that the employment of female pilots is contrary to the policy of of this company.'

'Contrary to the policy?' she repeated. 'You mean, you never employ women, not under any circumstances whatsoever?'

'We employ women as cabin staff—stewardesses, for example.'

Faun stared at him, her anger growing with every moment that passed.

'Can I ask why you have this aversion to women pilots, Mr Greenway?'

'It's the boss's decision, I'm afraid.' He stopped, and a small sigh escaped him. 'Yes,' he resumed, his pale eyes fixed once more on her completed application form lying on his blotter, 'it's his decision and therefore one that must be adhered to. Mr Tarrant would never consent to a woman's being in control of one of our aircraft. They're the last thing in luxury, as you know, and in consequence are extremely costly to buy.'

'Does Mr Tarrant conclude that, if a woman pilots one, it's more likely to end up as a pile of rubble at the end of a runway than if a man pilots it?' Deep sarcasm edged her tone, but she was merely assuming a front. Bitter disappointment flooded her whole being and she knew that she would be a long while getting over it. There was no doubt in her mind that if the decision had been left to Mr Greenway then the post would have been hers. And, she thought bitterly, had she been a man the post would have been hers. She said, although in a hopeless tone, 'What about the Sex Discrimination Act?'

'I rather expected you to bring that up,' rejoined Mr Greenway mildly. 'I suppose you could make a complaint, but I assure you, Miss Sheridan, that when Mr Tarrant makes a decision, there is little that could move him.'

Faun looked at him, noting again the signs of ill-health. She felt sorry for him, was sure that he too was disappointed that she was not to get the job.

'I shan't make a complaint,' she said tautly. 'But I only hope, Mr Greenway, that one day I shall meet this Mr Tarrant, and be able to give him a piece of my mind!'

'I do understand how you feel,' sympathised the personnel officer. 'But as I've said, Mr Tarrant will never sanction the employment of women pilots.'

'Mr Tarrant's obviously a man with outdated ideas regarding the inferiority of women,' she said tartly and, to her surprise, Mr Greenway instantly agreed with her.

'Yes, Miss Sheridan, unfortunately he is.'

Her mouth compressed as, for a moment, she paused in indecision. She could ask to speak to this Mr Clive Tarrant now, and tell him exactly what she thought of him and his antiquated ideas. Yes, she *would* ask to see

14

him! But she was told that he was away at present, and in any case he would refuse to see her—or any other applicant, for that matter.

'These things are left entirely in my hands,' went on Mr Greenway, whose tone was now one of finality. The interview was at an end.

'I warned you, dear.' Her mother's words did nothing to assuage the bitterness which Faun was experiencing over the loss of the job on which she had set her heart. 'It's plain that you're dreadfully disappointed.'

'I'm more angry than disappointed at this moment. How I wish I could meet up with that pompous, male-opinionated creature who considers us inferior! I hate him!' added Faun almost savagely. 'Even though I've never set eyes on him!'

'That's rather strong, dear.' Mrs Sheridan, her face troubled, placed a comforting hand on her daughter's shoulder. 'Getting yourself into a rage isn't going to help,' she pointed out reasonably. 'After all, that isn't the only job of its kind.'

'But it happens to be the one that I wanted. *The* one!' Faun gritted her teeth, forming a mental picture of a man whose whole appearance spelled arrogance and superiority—a tall, angular man with a cynical outlook on life and a contemptuous attitude towards women. 'I expect,' she added, diverting from the actual picture for a moment, 'that he's frustrated—he was probably crossed in love in his youth!'

Her mother's eyes widened; she seemed to be suppressing a smile as she murmured, in tones designed to be soothing,

'I shouldn't trouble yourself over him, dear, or his probable misfortunes.'

'Now you're being sarcastic,' complained Faun in an injured voice. The picture returned and she added to it. The man had a thin unattractive mouth, a smile that was in reality a sneer. He probably drank a lot, she thought, and his face would reveal the fact.

'Not at all,' protested Mrs Sheridan. 'I'm merely pointing out the futility of wasting your time on the wretched man.'

After a moment of frowning silence Faun nodded in agreement.

'You're quite right, darling, as always. Oh, but I can't help being furious!'

'It's understandable that you should be, but the sooner you put the miserable business out of your mind the better.'

'It's so galling,' went on Faun, unable to drop the subject even though she had agreed that there was nothing to be gained by pursuing it. 'Why should any man be like that in these enlightened times? I'm working at present; one of the world's largest airlines is willing for me to fly its planes, to accept the responsibility of the safety of its passengers, so why can't he? He *must* have been crossed in love in his youth!' she repeated. 'There can be no other reason for his dislike of women, can there?'

'Faun, dear,' began her mother a trifle impatiently, 'the fact that he objects to female pilots in no way proves he's a woman-hater, which is what you're trying to say.'

'I'm sure I'm right.'

'Nonsene! And another thing, what makes you assume that he's an old man?'

'His Victorian ideas,' replied Faun instantly. 'He's a soured old man with a grudge against our sex.'

Despite her growing impatience Mrs Sheridan had to laugh.

'You are in a state, aren't you? I'll tell you what—we'll all go out to dinner this evening. It's high time your father gave us a treat.'

Faun managed to smile then, just to please her mother. But inwardly she still brooded. It was ridiculous that she had lost her job simply because Clive Tarrant, the power behind the firm, harboured such old-fashioned ideas about women.

It was just ten days later that Faun received a letter bearing the printed symbol which she instantly recognised.

'It's from Mr Greenway,' she frowned, slitting the envelope open. 'I never expected to hear from him again.'

'Mr Greenway?' repeated Mrs Sheridan, for the moment puzzled. 'Who's he?'

'The man who interviewed me for that job ...' Faun's voice trailed off as, having opened the letter, she began to read its contents.

'You've got the job, after all!' exclaimed her mother excitedly as she saw Faun's expression change. 'Let me see!' And, moving quickly towards her, she looked over Faun's shoulder. 'But it isn't from Mr Greenway,' she pointed out, indicating the signature at the end. 'It's from a Maurice Slater. Did you meet him that day?'

Faun shook her head bewilderedly.

'I can't understand it,' she breathed, her heartbeats increasing with excitement as she read on. 'There must be some mistake,' she added, just as if she had to, because the news was too good to be true.

'Mistake? There's no mistake that I can see.' Mrs Sheridan pointed to a particular passage in the letter, and read it aloud '... you are hereby invited to attend for an air check. On successful completion of this, and subject to a satisfactory written examination and medical, we shall be pleased to inform you of the success of your application for the post of co-pilot—navigator with the above company.'

'I just can't believe it!' Faun shook her head, recalling the latter part of the interview, and the finality with which she had been told that Clive Tarrant would never sanction the employment of women pilots in his firm. 'I wonder why it's signed by this other man?'

Her mother merely gave a shrug of her shoulders.

'Is that important? The important thing is that you've managed to get the job, after all. I expect Mr Greenway's on holiday, or something.'

'But he was so emphatic about women not being employed. At that time Mr Tarrant would never have taken me on; I'm sure of it.'

'Do you know what I think?' said her mother. 'After Mr Greenway had spoken to him and given him a full account of your qualifications Mr Tarrant saw at once that you'd be a great asset to his firm and decided you were far too valuable to lose.'

Faun had to smile. There was not a mother in England who had more pride in her daughters' achievements than Mrs Sheridan.

'It would seem that yet again you're right.' Turning, Faun hugged her affectionately. 'And I'm glad you are! Hurrah! I'm so happy I could burst!'

'Darling Faun!' Mrs Sheridan shuddered and assumed a pained expression. 'How indelicate you are at times. Quite a dual personality you have.'

Faun laughed.

'No such thing,' she protested, her voice as light as air. 'You're always saying that.'

Her mother sighed and shook her head.

'It's true, Faun, and you know it, deep down inside you. You like to be considered tough—the super-efficient pilot of aeroplanes, the woman who's chosen to do a man's job, just as your sister did, becoming one of the first woman engineers specialising in her particular field of industry. But unlike Jean you're not in the least tough. You're very feminine, and vulnerable—No, don't interrupt. I'm having my say this time.'

'You always do,' Faun could not resist inserting with a mischievous grin. 'You've tyrannised over the three of us for as long as I can remember.'

'Rubbish!' But Mrs Sheridan responded to her daughter's grin before reverting to what she had been saying before the interruption. 'Yes, you're vulnerable, and I often worry about you. Up till now, for example, you've never been in love.'

'I've had no time,' laughed Faun, then added with a grimace, 'And now that I've got this marvellous job there certainly won't be any time.'

'You only want to be a career girl?' The edge of anxiety to her mother's voice troubled Faun and she frowned. 'You've no desire for any of the more natural pleasures of life?'

19

Unwilling to argue, or to hurt her mother in any way, Faun merely replied by saying that if love was to come her way, all well and good; if not, then she would be quite content with the life fate had planned for her. The subject was then closed and during the silence which followed Faun once again perused the letter.

'I'll telephone the company,' she decided, as she was not altogether satisfied with the way the business had turned out. She had a feeling of anxiety that something might be wrong.

A few minutes later she was speaking to Mr Greenway's secretary, learning that the personnel officer was in hospital, having suffered a stroke while at work. He was still in a coma.

'Mr Slater has taken over his duties,' added the young woman. 'He has written to you already. You received his letter?'

'Yes, today.' Faun paused thoughtfully. 'When did Mr Greenway have this stroke?'

'The day following the interviews.'

'I see.' Faun expressed her regret for Mr Greenway's illness but spoke mechanically, aware that her misgivings had some foundation; something was wrong. But as yet it was all a puzzle. Perhaps if she spoke to Mr Slater she would be given some enlightenment. 'Can I come into the office this afternoon?' she inquired at length.

'If it's important.'

'It's about my appointment,' returned Faun guardedly.

'You're attending for the air check next week. You were advised of this in the letter you received.'

20

'Yes.' Faun paused, her heart racing. That a major error had occurred was plain, an error resulting from Mr Greenway's indisposition and the confusion which would naturally follow. It would appear that she, Faun, could benefit by this confusion ... so why should she not take a chance?

'That's really all that's important,' the secretary was saying, 'the air check.'

'I'd still like to come in this afternoon, if Mr Slater can see me?' Faun asked if Mr Tarrant was still away from the office and was told that he was in the island of Bali at present.

'And we don't seem able to contact him,' added the girl.

Not in contact with the man who really mattered ...

'Will Mr Slater see me, do you think?'

'I should have to ask him. I'll do this and ring you back.' She asked for the number and was given it by Faun. The next moment the receiver clicked at the other end of the line. Faun held hers for a long reflective interlude before replacing it on its rest. Mr Greenway was in a coma, the girl had told her. Faun felt a sudden tingling of nerves, the result of excitement. Mr Greenway had definitely not intended offering her the job; in fact he had told her frankly that it was not in his power to do so. Yet she *had* been offered the job ... but only because Mr Greenway was not occupying his usual position as personnel officer.

CHAPTER TWO

SHE arrived at the office at ten to three, having been granted an interview with Mr Slater for three o'clock. Five minutes later she was sitting in his office, having been conducted there by one of the clerks. Mr Slater was not there, though the odour of his pipe hung heavily on the air and the clerk assured her that he was not very far away. When he did arrive, at a couple of minutes past three, he smilingly apologised for keeping her waiting.

'That's all right,' she returned quickly. 'I was a little early.'

'Now,' he began briskly when he was seated on the opposite side of the desk, 'what can I do for you?'

She hesitated, held back by the difficulty of finding the right words. However, Mr Slater saved her the trouble as he said how delighted he was to meet her, and how happy everyone was at the appointment of a woman pilot at last.

'You know about Mr Greenway's sudden illness, of course,' he continued, appearing to have forgotten all about the question he had put to her. This suited Faun, since she was being afforded the opportunity of enlightenment as to what had transpired in Mr Greenway's absence. In this way she would probably learn of the circumstances under which the job had been offered to her after all the personnel manager had said.

'Yes,' she replied. 'I was told about it when I telephoned. It's very sad indeed. Will he be all right eventually?' She eyed Mr Slater as she spoke, taking in the round jovial face, which shone as if recently well-soaped. The brown eyes looked straight into hers; the bushy brows below wispy hair gave him a homely, benign appearance. She decided she liked this man, just as she had liked Mr Greenway. The girl who had shown her into the office was also a charming person and it seemed to Faun that the boss must inevitably be an alien in such pleasing company.

'He's very ill indeed,' answered Mr Slater regretfully. 'Still in a coma, went into it while I was there, at the hospital, trying to discover which one of you had been given the job.'

Faun's nerve-ends prickled; she ventured guardedly, 'He told you he had offered it to me?'

'That's right. And you are ready for the air check next week? You can get time off?'

'Yes, that will be all right. My employers are most helpful and understanding.'

'You seem confident, but then who wouldn't be with your background?'

Faun said still in guarded tones,

'Weren't you surprised at the appointment of a woman?'

'Surprised?' he echoed, brows raised. 'I was astounded, and even decided that Kenneth was delirious— the nurse warned me that he would be, but he was perfectly rational, I can assure you.'

Faun, who knew full well that she had *not* been given the job, continued to put her questions cautiously.

'What about the attitude of Mr Tarrant?'

23

'The boss? There again I was astounded. That he would ever relent seemed impossible, but Kenneth convinced me that when he heard of your capabilities, Mr Tarrant said immediately that you must be offered the job.'

'He did?' Flashing in her alert mind was a picture— she always had formed pictures of people and situations; sometimes they proved to be correct, but inevitably they were sometimes out. The picture this time was of the hospital ward, of the man in the bed talking to his colleague about the applicants for the post of co-pilot with his company. The man in the bed appeared to be sufficiently rational, but Faun knew instinctively that he was not—that he was in fact rambling, saying what he would have *liked* to say, and not what he *should* have said.

That he admired the woman applicant was without question; that it was his personal wish for her to have the job also went without question. Faun could imagine this playing on his mind even before he had had the stroke, could visualise his frustration at his inability to appoint her, for it was now obvious to her that not only the personnel manager but everyone else in the office favoured the appointment of women as pilots. In his ramblings Kenneth Greenway had said what, in the very beginning, he had wished he could say: that Mr Tarrant had relented and therefore the job had been given to the woman applicant.

Only one question puzzled her. Where was the man Mr Greenway *had* chosen for the job? Suddenly Faun had the answer. No one had been chosen—because no one had possessed the qualifications demanded by the

24

company. No one with the exception of *herself*. This fitted in with Faun's conviction that Mr Greenway would most definitely have chosen her, had it been within his power to do so. She returned her attention to Mr Slater as he replied to her question.

'Yes, Miss Sheridan, Mr Tarrant has offered you the job. As I've said, this news astounded me—as it did the rest of the staff here.'

'Mr Tarrant ... He wasn't here when I had the interview.'

'He wasn't in the office—no.' Appearing to be faintly puzzled by the irrelevancy of her statement, Mr Slater stared questioningly at her.

'Mr Greenway was able to get in touch with him later, then?'

'Obviously. He had not then decided to go to Bali, of course. He's there at the present time—but I understand Mr Greenway's secretary informed you of this during your telephone conversation with her. It's a pity you won't be seeing him yet awhile.'

Faun said nothing to this. The last person she wanted to see at present was the detestable boss of the exclusive Tarrant Line! Her thoughts returned to what Mr Slater had said earlier, and she saw that it all fitted in with the picture she had formed, with the theory she had come to regarding the ramblings of Mr Greenway. There was no doubt in her mind that Mr Tarrant had *not* been consulted, simply because Mr Greenway knew it would be pointless to ask him to take on a woman pilot. How very convincing the personnel manager must have been, though, to deceive Mr Slater in this way.

'The young lady I spoke to on the telephone said you

hadn't any contact with Mr Tarrant at present.' Faun spoke casually, though she was filled with elation at the turn of events. Once she was employed by the firm, she could not be dismissed—not with the law as it now stood. 'Do you know how long he will be away?'

Mr Slater shrugged his shoulders, glancing at the ceiling as if to gain enlightenment there.

'It could be as long as a couple of months; he's combining business with pleasure. He's an idea he might open an hotel there.'

'In Bali? How exciting!'

'A truly beautiful island, so we are given to believe. Mr Tarrant's been there several times.' He paused a moment. 'It's quite true that we are unable to get in touch with him, but this is not altogether unusual. He has interests in that part of the world and could in fact be travelling to somewhere like Bangkok or some other place around that quarter.'

Faun was not particularly interested in what Mr Slater was now saying. Rather was her mind on the duration of time the boss would be away—two months. Time to prove her merit to the man whose opinion of women was so small! Yes, she would show him she could do as well as any of his other pilots!

'Shall you have to work a month's notice?' Mr Slater was inquiring presently.

'No; my employers know I've applied for this job and they are willing to release me—if it should be necessary, that is?' She looked interrogatingly at him, saw him shake his head.

'I don't think there's any real urgency, Miss Sheridan. However, you just go on and arrange things to suit yourself. We're able to take you on immediately you've satisfied us with your air check, and the exams mentioned in the letter.'

'I haven't given this part of it much thought yet,' began Faun, then turned her head as the door opened and a young man stood there. He instantly apologised for the intrusion.

'I didn't know you were engaged, Maurice,' he added, preparing to withdraw. Mr Slater gestured him to come forward.

'This is Miss Sheridan, our first lady pilot. Miss Sheridan—Patrick Goulding, one of our co-pilots.'

'Lord,' ejaculated the young man, staring at her in amazement, 'how old are you?'

'What a tactless question to ask a lady,' chided Mr Slater. 'I should ignore it, Miss Sheridan.'

Faun laughed and said,

'I'm older than I look, Mr Goulding.'

'You must be! If you weren't you'd still be in the schoolroom!'

Another laugh escaped her.

'Thank you, Mr Goulding. I really must consider buying myself a white wig and some spectacles.'

Grinning, he came closer, and stood looking down at her.

'I wouldn't bother. I like you as you are.'

Faun said nothing. Having received this sort of compliment so many times before, she was beginning to find it rather stale. She was wondering why the pilot had not been more surprised by her appointment, but suddenly realised that this must already have been much discussed by all the members of the airline staff.

27

'Can I offer you my congratulations?' Patrick Goulding was saying. 'You've done an amazing thing, but I expect you know that already?'

'Miss Sheridan is fully aware that her impressive record has broken down the boss's aversion to women. She deserves a medal, don't you think?'

'Indeed yes! I still find it almost impossible to believe the miracle's been worked. Clive's been so dogmatic about the unreliability of women in general. You've made a remarkable break-through, Miss Sheridan.'

'She certainly has,' agreed Mr Slater enthusiastically.

Although interested in all this interchange Faun had her mind fixed mainly on the more serious side of the situation. That she was running a risk did not for a moment escape her. For although she had told herself that she could not be sacked, she was not at all sure that Clive Tarrant would not, somehow, contrive to get rid of her. She would then be out of a job, having thrown up the excellent job she had at the present time. For a fleeting moment caution told her to hold on to this job, but soon she was seeing the challenge presented to her. She just had to prove to the detestable Clive Tarrant that she was more than capable of handling his aeroplanes.

The two men were talking and the word eccentric caught her ear.

'I can't agree with you that he's eccentric,' Mr Slater was saying with a frown, 'just because he likes to disappear for a while, to get away from the worries of the business. When he's here he never lets up, as you know.' Patrick Goulding said nothing to this and Mr Slater added with a grin, 'I'd do the same were I in his position. After all, he does have his *chère amie* with him.'

'He has a girl-friend?' ejaculated Faun without stopping to think. 'At his age!'

'His age?' blinked Patrick. 'How old do you think he is, for heaven's sake?'

She coloured, realising just how absurd her interruption was.

'I've no idea,' she answered lamely, flickering a glance in Mr Slater's direction and seeing that he too wore an expression of surprise. 'I somehow gained the impression that he was getting on in years.'

'Well, I don't know how,' said Mr Slater.

'He wouldn't be very pleased to hear it.' Patrick Goulding looked at Faun with a hint of amusement in his eyes. 'Clive's just on thirty-four, Miss Sheridan—and handsome with it!'

'He is?' So her picture of him had flaws, it would seem.

'Very. A most attractive man is our boss. The tall, lithe outdoor type, bronzed and all the rest that appeals to the fair sex,' he added with a laugh. 'He's a pilot himself, incidentally. Had a short-term commission in the R.A.F.' Patrick Goulding would have added to this, but Mr Slater, glancing at his watch, brought the conversation to an end, saying apologetically,

'You'll have to excuse me, Miss Sheridan, but I've an appointment in five minutes' time.' He smiled at her and made some casual remark about the air-check she was soon to be taking. Then, with both the men wish-

29

ing her luck, Faun left the office and drove herself home.

The air-check and examination were over; the medical had been taken the day previously, given by Faun's own doctor, and now she was sitting in the office of the deputy managing director of the Tarrant Line, a little tired, but well pleased with her efforts. Sitting in front of her was a tall thin man who had introduced himself as Mr Norton.

'Nice to meet you, Miss Sheridan,' he began, then went on to tell her he had heard all about her from Mr Slater. She was perfectly composed, waiting to hear that the job was hers. This she did hear, with the added words,

'On behalf of Mr Tarrant, may I welcome you to the staff of the famous Tarrant Line? As you know, the boss is away at present, but undoubtedly he'll be delighted to make your acquaintance when he eventually arrives back in England.'

Faun looked away, hiding her expression. It could be funny, this situation in which she found herself—could turn out to be a comedy of errors with a happy ending ... but she very much had her doubts. Whether she would eventually come to the point where she could look forward to the meeting with her new boss was debatable. For the present, she would not care if he stayed on in Bali for the rest of his life!

'If there's nothing else ...' Faun looked at Mr Norton across the desk. She was eager to get home and tell her mother the news.

'You want to be going——?' He stopped, frowning,

as a knock sounded on the office door. 'Come in,' he said abruptly, and a moment later he was being handed a note by a young lady he had addressed as Miss Bruce. The girl spoke to Faun softly as Mr Norton read the note.

'Congratulations, Miss Sheridan. We still can't believe you've done it!'

Faun merely acknowledged this with a smile, foreseeing a nine days' wonder if Clive Tarrant should remain adamant even though she had proved her worth.

'How many crews have we out at the moment?' Mr Norton's frown had deepened; it was clear that some kind of a crisis had occurred.

'All except one.'

'We shall need that one in a hurry.'

'I've already called them in.'

'The devil you have!' Mr Norton gave her a glance of admiration. 'What a pleasure it is to have a super-efficient staff about me.'

'A Colles' fracture,' mused Miss Bruce with a grimace. 'He'll be as mad as a bull, I shouldn't wonder.'

'Never known him to be laid up before.'

Mr Norton looked at Faun, and his mind was recalled to her desire to leave. He smiled and told her she could go, which she did at once, promising to let him know the exact date when she could take up her duties with the firm.

Her mother was quite naturally delighted, and yet Faun sensed a hint of anxiety about her and knew that she was thinking that her daughter would be so wrapped up in this new job that she'd have no time for men and romance. Marriage for both Faun and

31

Jean was what Mrs Sheridan really wanted; she envied her friends who had grandchildren coming to see them at the week-ends.

Faun's father was happy indeed; he saw no reason why his two daughters should not remain career girls if they so wished.

'You didn't have ideas like that when you persistently badgered me to marry you!' was his wife's tart rejoinder when he was unwise enough to mention how he felt about Faun's new appointment. 'You didn't care a toss that I was giving up such a promising career!'

'Have you ever regretted it, dear?'

'You know I haven't—and therein lies the strength of my argument regarding my daughters. If they find the right sort of husbands they'll never regret giving it all up for marriage.'

'Shall we change the subject, pet?' suggested Faun with a little laugh. 'If the right one comes along then I promise you I'll give him my most careful consideration.'

'If you take that sort of businesslike attitude then you'll frighten him away!'

'Tell me,' said Mr Sheridan, deciding to change the subject before his daughter became impatient, 'when do you start with the Tarrant Line?'

'I can start as soon as I like.'

'You can?' he said, considering. 'I would advise you to start right away, then.'

She nodded. Her employers had offered to release her and so there were no obstacles to her taking up the job at once. More time to show her worth, she thought, little knowing that fate was soon to take a hand and that she was not to have that two months after all.

It was early evening three days later when the plane began its approach to Denpasar airfield. The runway lights were in view and Faun made her final transmission to the tower, informing the authorities that they were about to land. After landing, the aircraft was prepared for the following day's flight and then the crew took a taxi to the Bali Beach hotel where Clive Tarrant was staying, with his girl-friend.

In the taxi Faun tried not to think of the coming interview with her formidable boss, and managed to do so, but only by reflecting on the events leading up to this flight to the island of Bali.

She had told her employers she had got the job, asked for immediate release and been given it. Two days later she had taken up her duties with Tarrant Line and immediately learned that the man who had injured his wrist was none other than Clive Tarrant himself, who had suffered the accident as a result of surf-riding off the beautiful Sanur Beach.

The next thing Faun knew was that the crew designated to bring him home were a man short, as the co-pilot had gone sick.

'You can take his place,' said Mr Norton casually. 'It would seem you're to meet your boss much sooner than you expected.'

Faun's heart had sunk; she could see herself out of work within the next few days. If only she had been given that two months—or one month, even ... Now, she knew it was most unlikely that she would be able to keep the job she had set her heart upon right from the moment of reading the advertisement.

'The boss isn't going to be pleased at the delay,' Malcolm Devonshire had commented at the start of the trip. 'We'd have gone out the day before yesterday, but Joe was off-colour. We waited—had to, because there wasn't anyone to take his place as every other crew had assignments for the next week or so. Joe made no improvement and in fact he's now in bed, and his wife has sent for the doctor.'

Malcolm was speaking to her now, as he sat beside her in the back of the taxi.

'Thanks, Faun, for a most pleasant trip. Mr Norton said you were good and you are.' He spoke with sincerity and Faun knew that the prejudice against women pilots was plainly dying. If only she could convince Clive Tarrant that she was as good as any man ... But her opportunity had gone, and she chafed against her bad luck in being forced to meet him much sooner than would otherwise had been the case.

A little cough from the captain reminded her that he was expecting a comment. She turned to him with a ready smile, thanking him for letting her fly the plane.

'I really did enjoy that leg from Bombay to Calcutta,' she added. 'Thank you very much.'

The hotel was reached, a luxurious building with its palm-shaded grounds coming right down to the Sanur Beach. Much travelled though she was, Faun had never seen anything quite like this exotic setting, with the smooth coral sands and the clear aquamarine sea caressing the shore.

Malcolm made himself known at the reception desk; he was handed a message, grimacing as he read it.

'We're to see the boss as soon as we arrive,' he told Faun and the steward. Faun's pulse quickened even though she had marshalled all her courage, assuring herself she was ready to meet the boss, and to do battle with him if necessary.

'Can I wash and change first?'

'I expect so,' replied Malcolm obligingly. 'We'll meet here, in the lobby, in about twenty minutes' time. Okay?'

She nodded, although she would have preferred a little longer. A shower would not have come amiss, she thought, but it would have to come later.

Promptly at the appointed time she was back in the lobby. She had changed into a sleeveless cotton dress of a pretty flowered design; her long chestnut hair fell luxuriously on to her shoulders, giving a very feminine effect, and she thought rather dejectedly that she looked exceedingly young as well.

'Come on,' smiled Malcolm, his appreciative gaze settling on her lovely face for a second or two. 'Let's see how the invalid is.'

The suite of rooms occupied by Clive Tarrant and his girl-friend was the last thing in luxury, and one of the most expensive suites in the hotel, Faun later learned. The sitting-room into which she and the two other crew members entered had a balcony facing the gardens, the shore and the sea beyond. But for the moment this delightful view was lost on Faun as she looked at the man sitting in a chair by another window, which was wide open. In one glance she took in the crisp, light-brown hair, shining and inclined to wave, the straight eyebrows and deep-set blue eyes beneath lazy, hooded lids. These eyes were piercing and hard as metal. The features were aquiline, the skin clear and deeply tanned. High cheekbones gave an angular aspect to his face, and a quality of ruthlessness. The mouth was thin and yet there was a certain sensuousness about it which convinced Faun that the man was by no means as cold and unemotional as she would have expected.

'Hello, Ingrid.' Malcolm greeted Clive Tarrant's girl-friend with a faint smile before turning his attention to Clive Tarrant himself. 'Sorry to see you all plastered like this——' He waved a hand, indicating the plaster which went from Clive's wrist to his elbow.

'Cut out the corny jokes. Where's Joe? And who is this?' His insolent glance flickered to Faun, then back to Malcolm. 'What kept you? I expected you two days ago.' His glance moved to Tommy, the steward, who was standing by the door. 'You can go,' he said, and the young man departed—probably with a sigh of relief, thought Faun, as it was plain that the boss was not in the best of moods.

'Joe's sick; that's what caused the delay, as there was only our crew available when your message came through. However, Miss Sheridan came to us, which was fortunate for you, since we wouldn't have been here yet if she hadn't. Miss Sheridan, meet the boss, Clive Tarrant.'

Clive Tarrant merely nodded impatiently, scarcely noticing when Faun said, marvelling at the steadiness of her voice, 'How do you do, Mr Tarrant?'

'For the lord's sake be more explicit,' he commanded, almost glowering at Malcolm. 'If Joe's sick then who came with you?'

'Who ...?' Malcolm looked at him as if he doubted his sanity. 'Miss Sheridan, of course. Haven't I just said so?'

Faun decided it was time she spoke; on this occasion, however, her voice was far from steady.

'I'm the new co-pilot, Mr Tarrant. I stood in for Joe——'

'The——!' It was Ingrid who uttered the exclamation. Clive Tarrant was merely staring at Faun, obviously lost for words. 'You're crazy!' continued Ingrid. 'Clive never employs women pilots. Malcolm, what's this all about?'

Clive Tarrant turned his attention to her. One look seemed to deflate the girl, for she moved over to a chair and sat down, her cheeks tinged with crimson.

'Malcolm,' said Clive Tarrant in a very soft tone, 'I'm in no mood for riddles. I've asked you to be more explicit?'

The captain, obviously aware now that all was not right, looked bewilderedly from his boss to Faun. She was pale, but tolerably composed. She knew she must speak to Clive Tarrant in private and was waiting an opportunity to request this. The girl, Ingrid, was watching her keenly, though she ventured no comment, still smarting as she was under the admonishing glance she had received from Clive Tarrant.

Malcolm spoke at length, his voice edged with anxiety.

'Miss Sheridan is, as she's told you, our new co-pilot.

She started with us yesterday and was able to come with me ...' His voice trailed off. 'Something's radically wrong, isn't it?'

For a long and awful silence Faun and Clive Tarrant stared at one another. Then he said, still in that same soft tone of voice,

'Miss Sheridan——' He stopped, shaking his head as if totally bewildered. 'Perhaps you will explain what this is all about?' The blue eyes flickered over her with more interest than before, taking in, she felt sure, how young she looked, and how little fitted to handle an aeroplane.

'It's quite true, Mr Tarrant,' said Faun quietly. 'I am working for you, as a pilot. This is my first trip with your firm——'

'How the devil did you land the job,' broke in Malcolm, 'if Clive knew nothing about it?'

Clive's eyes slid to his.

'Yes,' he murmured in a very soft tone, 'how the devil did she land the job?'

'We all believed that you had sanctioned her appointment.'

'Then you're all fools.' The voice remained soft as Clive Tarrant added, 'Miss Sheridan, you appear to know all the answers, so get on with it!'

Faun swallowed, as a little ball of anger had settled in her throat. She requested that she speak to him in private, but he shook his head.

'Get on with it,' he repeated, his hard eyes boring into her.

She glared at him.

'Only if you do as I ask,' she said tautly, 'will you be put fully in the picture.'

'Faun,' interposed Malcolm in a pleading voice, 'what in heaven's name is this all about?'

'Are you issuing me with an ultimatum?' inquired Clive Tarrant, ignoring the captain's question.

'If you see it that way, Mr Tarrant, then yes, it is an ultimatum.'

A gasp from Ingrid, and a visible start by Malcolm. Faun, still pale but composed, waited for Clive Tarrant to make up his mind. The icy glow in his eyes, the tightness of his mouth, the little drifts of crimson creeping up the sides of his jaw ... all these denoted the fury that was rising within him. Faun would have wagered her last penny that no one had ever issued an ultimatum to him before. Well, a new experience would do him no harm, she thought, her eyes sliding for the moment to the girl. Slinky, would be how her mother would describe Ingrid's figure. She was tall, and superbly dressed in a trouser-suit of fine white linen. Her dark hair was immaculate, her skin clear and creamy. She had very full lips, and wide, a long neck around which was a gold necklace made of little stars; in the centre of each was a small diamond. A present from Clive? wondered Faun, her glance returning to him in time to see him make an imperative gesture with his hand. Malcolm turned stiffly and opened the door; Ingrid made no move to leave her chair, but Clive Tarrant said harshly,

'Leave us!' and she got up at once, following Malcolm as he left the room. 'Well?' encouraged Clive softly as soon as the door was closed.

Faun moved towards a chair.

'May I sit down?' she asked, pointedly reminding him of his omission. He seemed to grit his teeth, though his voice was quiet and suave when he replied,

'By all means, Miss Sheridan.'

'Thank you.' Sedately she took possession of the chair, smoothing her dress before beginning to speak. She heard his indrawn breath of impatience but ignored it. When she did presently begin to explain he made no interruption at all until she said,

'Of course, I realised a mistake had been made——'

'But you carried on regardless?'

'It was a challenge, Mr Tarrant. I felt that, with two months in which to prove my capabilities, I had the sort of advantage which would serve me in good stead.'

'Then you were wrong, Miss Sheridan.'

She looked at him with a frank and direct stare.

'I can prove to you that I'm as capable as any other of your pilots.'

He was shaking his head even before she had finished speaking.

'You can prove no such thing,' he said.

'You're not intending to give me the opportunity?'

He smiled then, a detestable smile.

'This time you *are* right, Miss Sheridan. I am not intending to give you the opportunity.'

'Why?' she queried briefly and with a curt edge to her voice.

'Miss Sheridan,' he said in measured tones, 'I am not in the habit of having my decisions questioned by a member of my staff.'

'Am I a member of your staff?' she countered, unable to resist seizing this opportunity of forcing a direct answer from him.

'No, Miss Sheridan, you are not.'

'In that case,' she reasoned, not without a glimmer of a smile, 'I *am* able to question your decision, yes?'

The blue eyes narrowed to slits.

'No one,' he returned arrogantly, 'ever questions my decisions.'

Faun's eyes were kindling.

'There is now a law in our country, Mr Tarrant, which goes by the name of the Sex Discrimination Act. You are no longer allowed to favour either sex when seeking an employee.'

Clive Tarrant was now evincing a small degree of humour.

'I had expected this to come,' he said with maddening calm. 'Make no mistake, Miss Sheridan, I'm more than capable of removing you from my firm.'

She was sure of it, too. This man would never be dictated to, not by anyone at all. Of course, she could put up a fight, but even if she did manage to come out on top, she had no illusions about her ability to remain with his firm. As he had so confidently asserted, he would remove her. She said at last, hoping to keep the dejection out of her voice,

'Am I to take it that I no longer work for your company, Mr Tarrant?'

Faintly he inclined his head.

'*You* are correct, Miss Sheridan,' he replied inexorably.

She paused a while, but with nothing to lose she decided to give him the set-down he deserved.

'In that case,' she said, 'I'm in a position to tell you exactly what I think about you.' She stopped, awaiting his reaction in the form of a cutting rejoinder, but although some kind of emotion was stirred within him —betrayed by the slow pulsation of a nerve in the side of his cheek—his face remained an unreadable mask. 'In my opinion,' she continued, 'you're a pompous, arrogant, self-opinionated fool——'

'Fool!' he ejaculated, and she knew that this one word had really found its mark. 'Why, you——!'

'Yes,' she broke in, determined to have her full say, 'fool! You're a fool to yourself for not retaining the services of a person who has all the qualifications you require—and more—*more*, Mr Tarrant!'

'You know how to blow your own trumpet, that's for sure.' Clive Tarrant's voice was surprisingly controlled as he added, 'There's a saying that self-praise is no recommendation.'

'I was not indulging in self-praise, Mr Tarrant. I was stating a fact.'

Clive looked contemptuously at her.

'You've certainly got an inflated opinion of yourself,' he sneered. 'However, it so happens that these marvellous qualifications you say you have are of no interest to me. I've worked with women pilots and, by God, I'd not risk my life by allowing one to fly me!'

'Doesn't it ever occur to you that you're living about a hundred years behind the times? You ought to have lived when the Victorian father was ruling his household with a rod of iron!'

'And when a female like you would have been given a taste of his walking-stick on her backside.'

Colour rushed to Faun's face. If only she dared to slap that sneering mouth of his! Instead, she told him he was the rudest man she had ever met, and that one of the things he ought to learn was to guard his tongue.

'If you don't,' she warned quiveringly, 'it'll get you into a great deal of trouble!'

He laughed then, and rejoined with sardonic amusement,

'Riled, are you, by that mention of chastisement? Miss Sheridan, women like you would bring our world to ruin if you were given a free hand in things in general.'

'You don't appear to have read about the equality of the sexes. Women are in everything nowadays. My sister's an engineer.'

The cold blue eyes opened very wide.

'How very disappointing for your mother when she discovered she had brought *two* Amazons into the world.'

'You're detestable!'

'And you're just about the most unattractive female I've ever met.' His tones were quiet, his eyes glimmering with a sort of amused disdain. 'Why don't you women keep to your own territory?'

'The kitchen, Mr Tarrant?' Her eyes swept over him, then settled for a space on the plaster encasing his right arm. 'Or perhaps just that little area round the sink? Is that where you'd like to find every one of my sex?'

He laughed and replied whimsically,

'They'd certainly be safer there than trying to fly aeroplanes.'

'Trying?' She glanced scornfully at him. 'You're contemptible! You won't even allow yourself to think on logical lines. I *can* fly planes. I've just come from

43

one of the largest companies in the world.'

'I'm not interested in the mistakes made by other companies. While I'm in charge of the Tarrant Line no females will fly my planes.'

'Would you kindly stop referring to me as a female!' She was consumed by fury and wished she could have found a way of reducing his male egotism to the very dust.

'So you don't even consider yourself a female?' His straight brows lifted a fraction. 'You're still a female, despite your tendencies to jump into the male world of science.' His eyes, insolent and amused, rested on Faun's firm delectable curves. 'Yes, miss, you're a female all right.'

She went hot with embarrassment, yet at the same time she was able to fling at him,

'A more disgusting male than you I've never seen!' He said nothing, but his lips curved in a smile of sheer amusement. He was having fun at her expense, actually enjoying the diversion brought about by this word-sparring which was taking place between them. 'It's as well for the world as a whole that your particular despotic type is in the minority. In fact,' added Faun, her voice vibrating with wrath, 'your type is so unimportant as to be neglible in your effect on our society!'

'Despotic?' He coloured slightly. So another barb had found its mark, she thought, deriving extreme satisfaction from the knowledge. He shrugged his shoulders, as if he had noticed her satisfaction and was endeavouring to deflate it for her. 'I'm not in the least interested in what effect I might or might not have on society. In my own particular firm I give the orders, and they're obeyed. You knew by your own admission that Greenway wouldn't have given you the job had he been in his senses; he knew my wishes and was fully intending to adhere to them.'

Faun rose from the chair.

'I shall demand compensation,' she threatened.

'Compensation?' he echoed with a lift of his brows.

'I've given up an excellent job to come to your company.'

'By your own admission you've indulged in sharp practice.' The dryly-spoken challenge was accompanied by a shake of the head. 'I shouldn't cherish any wild dreams of compensation,' he advised. 'You're not entitled to any.'

She stood there, eyeing him with the greatest contempt.

'You're shirking your responsibilities as well as adopting this insufferable, egotistical attitude regarding the job itself?'

'I'm a businessman——' He stopped, then asked in a very soft tone what she was looking at him like that for.

'I'd like to bring your pride to the dust!' she replied.

'Be very careful,' recommended Clive Tarrant in a dangerously quiet voice, 'for if you aren't you might find yourself stranded on this island. I could flatly refuse to allow you on my plane, remember.'

'I expect I should get home,' retorted Faun, lifting her head. 'I'm not a pauper, Mr Tarrant. I've been earning a very high salary up till now.'

'A man's salary,' he murmured, and she answered, her voice soft and dignified,

'The salary for the job, Mr Tarrant. Equal pay ... of which you obviously don't approve.'

'You are quite right, I don't approve.'

'I wish,' she said with a sigh, 'we could part company now! The idea of having your company on that plane for all those hours appals me!'

His mouth compressed.

'I've warned you, we'll be parting company on this island!' Faun said nothing and he added curiously, 'I wonder what the Amazon would like to do at this moment?'

She was at the door by this time, but she swung round to face him.

'Would you really like to know?'

'I'd be most interested.' His lips twitched; the sardonic amusement that had edged his tone was reflected in his expression.

'I'd like to have you in my power for about five minutes or so.'

'Indeed?' He laughed outright. 'I'm afraid there's not the remotest possibility of that, Miss Sheridan.'

'Unfortunately, no.' She opened the door and went out without another word.

Insufferable, hateful creature! She could willingly have subjected him to some kind of barbaric torture!

CHAPTER THREE

THE plane soared up from the airfield at Bali, with Faun and Malcolm in the cockpit and Clive Tarrant, Ingrid and Tommy in the passenger cabin behind. Looking down at the string of islands stretching across the calm blue sea, Faun likened them to a necklace of gems nestling on a bed of indigo velvet. However, the chief occupation of her mind was the weather brief which they had received from the Met. Office at Bali just as they were preparing to take off for Singapore, which was the first leg of the trip from Bali to England. The brief had not been at all favourable and Malcolm had been inclined to delay the start of the trip, but he was overruled by his boss, who insisted on taking off.

'I have to say this, then——' Malcolm paused a moment as if choosing his words with care, conscious that he was speaking to his employer. However, he obviously failed to produce any tactful way of delivering his message and Faun heard him continue, 'The responsibility's all yours, Clive.'

'I accept it,' curtly and with a note of irritation in his voice. He was obviously in a foul mood, thought Faun, looking at him with disgust. Never had she met so hateful a specimen of manhood. He would make a most abominable invalid, and Faun could not for the life of her understand what the glamorous Ingrid could see in him. However, everyone to his or her own taste; there must be something about the detestable creature that appealed to the girl.

'We're likely to run into cumulo-nimbus, with the possibility of active thunderstorms,' Faun had warned Clive, but this did not even bring a comment from him. 'There would then be severe turbulence,' she had added for good measure, but again received no response. Now, she was more than a little troubled, but she remained silent, certain that any further warning from her would fall on deaf ears. Were she the captain of this plane she would immediately turn around and seek permission to land—Clive Tarrant or no Clive Tarrant. Boss of the airline he might be, and owner of this machine ... but always it was the captain who had command, full command. However, if Malcolm chose to give way to his boss then there was nothing that Faun could do about it.

Sitting on Malcolm's right hand, she gave herself over to private thought, reflecting with anger on a conversation she had accidentally overheard as, about to pass the door of Clive Tarrant's room ten minutes or so after her battle of words with him, she had stopped abruptly on hearing Malcolm mention her name, then she heard him add,

'You'd never fault her flying ability, Clive.'

'That's your opinion. As I've just said, you're not to give her a leg. I'm having no female flying me!'

'She'd fly the machine as well as you or I,' persisted Malcolm, and Faun's heart warmed to him—just as it froze when she even thought of Clive Tarrant. 'I'll personally guarantee you'd never fault her.'

48

'There's no need for any guarantee. She just doesn't fly that machine. She'll keep to the role of navigator; that's my final word.'

Crimson with fury, Faun had moved on without hearing any more. All she wanted was to get back to England and say goodbye to Clive Tarrant for ever.

'We're meeting the turbulence.' Malcolm's troubled voice brought Faun back to the present and she nodded in agreement.

'There's a big formation of cumulo-nimbus. We're in for trouble, that's for sure.' Using the search radar, Faun checked the front that was steadily building up. 'The front's extensive,' she said presently, a frown creasing her brow. 'A hundred to a hundred and thirty miles in length, I should estimate.' Glancing at the captain's profile, she saw that it was set and motionless. She herself was tense, profoundly anxious about the weather into which they were flying. 'Do we climb over it or do we go under it?' she was asking presently, but Malcolm, deep in concentration, appeared not to have heard her. Naturally he was troubled, and she wondered why he did not use his authority and insist on returning to Bali. However, the decision was entirely his and it would seem that he felt he could get the aircraft through safely. Faun thought of the man at the back, sitting there with his girl-friend and the steward. He was probably listening on the intercom to all that was being said in the cockpit, and should Malcolm make a decision that did not suit Clive, then Faun was sure he would interrupt, even though he had no right to do so, seeing that Malcolm's word was law.

'See if you can find a gap I can get through,' ordered

Malcolm at last and, re-tuning the radar, Faun immediately made the necessary search.

'There's a small gap about twenty degrees to port,' she said, tilting the radar in an attempt to focus the picture of the two cumulo-nimbus clouds. 'It's about three miles wide.'

'Three miles.' Malcolm pursed his lips. 'We might just make it.'

Faun again tilted her radar, seeing the two towers of cloud—the dark and threatening cumulo-nimbus which would presently join, closing the gap. At the moment, though, the gap was there, about three thousand feet high, and although the turbulence within the gap would most certainly be felt, there would not be the rapid updraught which always occurred in the centre of the cloud.

'Can we make it?' Faun was becoming doubtful. 'The gap's closing rather quickly. We won't get through,' she decided, frowning heavily as they approached the gap.

'I must try,' returned Malcolm, and Faun said no more. She was again wondering if Clive Tarrant had his headset on and was listening to their conversation. Yes, he would be listening, but what was he thinking?

Suddenly, shooting into the darkening sky was a vivid white flash, followed almost instantaneously by a clap of thunder. The aircraft, being in a region of severe turbulence, was being tossed about and Faun could only hope that those at the back were strapped in. She thought of the girl and wondered how she was taking all this.

Another brilliant flash, another clap of thunder; the

50

main lights went out, but the emergency lights came on immediately.

After a moment Faun said,

'The radio's not working and the compasses have stumbled.'

Malcolm gave a sharp exclamation. By now, thought Faun, he would surely have decided that he ought not to have allowed Clive Tarrant to make a decision that should have been his and his alone.

'So we've now no directional reference?'

'No, I'm afraid not ...' Faun's voice faded as Malcolm, putting a hand to his chest, uttered another sharp exclamation and she realised at once that both this and the first one were indications that he was in pain. No sooner had this fact struck her than she heard him say, in low and jerky tones,

'God, I've got the most agonising pain here——' His words broke as, throwing up a hand, he slumped forward in his seat, prevented from falling only by his harness. Faun's heartbeats quickened; she wasted no time on questions but instantly took command of the aircraft, her one and only thought being to get it out of this turbulence and into clear air. The altimeter and artificial horizon were still working and after checking the radar she decided to descend. She glanced at Malcolm, still slumped in his seat, motionless, as if he were dead. It would not be the first time a pilot had died in the cockpit, but it was the first time Faun had experienced anything like this, and it was frightening; this she had to admit. Her heart was throbbing wildly; her nerves would have played her up had she not determinedly kept a tight rein on them. She was in sole charge of the aircraft now that Malcolm was no longer able to fly it. She was the captain—the only person on board with the authority to issue orders. How was Clive Tarrant going to accept the situation? she wondered, hesitating for a moment before speaking to him on the intercom. She spoke quietly, gratified to discover that there was not even a trace of unsteadiness in her voice as she told Clive what had happened.

'Malcolm's unconscious!' he repeated, cutting in before she could make any reference to the lightning strike they'd received. 'What happened?'

'He just slumped over the controls. I'm now in charge,' she added—and would dearly have loved to see the detestable man's expression. 'I'm endeavouring to break through this front. Until I have there's nothing we can do for Malcolm.'

Clive agreed at once. With the aircraft being tossed about by the violent currents it was impossible either for him or the steward to discard their harness and come forward.

Under Faun's expert hands the aircraft was gradually brought from the turbulence into clear air, and at last Clive came forward, accompanied by Tommy.

'Is he ... dead?' asked Tommy in an awed voice. Clive, whose hand had slid to Malcolm's heart, announced that he was still breathing.

'We'll get the harness off and then take him to the passenger cabin. Tommy, move as quickly as you can; I'll do my best with my one good arm.' Clive spoke with quiet authority and Faun realised he had taken full command. She bit her lip, angry at the arrogance of his approach, yet at the same time she had to admit that this was certainly not the time to begin arguing out the point that she was the captain of the aircraft and, therefore, in full control. The lightning strike had been severe and Faun began at once to make a complete handling check in order to discover the extent of the damage to the aircraft. She was soon breathing freely, the machine's performance being satisfactory, much to her surprise.

Clive, although appearing to be giving his full attention to the stricken pilot, did refer to the lightning strike, asking what damage had been done to the machine.

'None that I can find. I've made the handling check and haven't come across any major faults—but I've no compass at this time.' She spoke in grave and quiet tones, wondering if his opinion of women pilots was undergoing any change as a result of what was happening, and the efficient manner in which she was carrying out her duties as captain of the aircraft. She cast him a sideways glance as he stood, at Malcolm's back, attempting to make some contribution to the loosening of the harness. Tommy was at the front, making good progress. Clive caught Faun's glance and said,

'So the performance is satisfactory?' His tone of authority riled her; she could have had some considerable difficulty with her temper had the situation not been so serious.

'Yes, from what I can see.'

Clive's mouth curved sardonically.

'Being cautious, eh?' His eyes laughed. 'Not committing yourself fully?'

'Would you commit yourself fully?' she challenged.

'Of course,' with egotistical confidence. 'I'd know for sure whether or not damage had been sustained.'

Faun counted ten, and then breathed out—slowly.

'Unfortunately we're not all as clever as you, Mr Tarrant.'

A silence followed and then, curtly and authoritatively,

'If the performance satisfies you then put the power on——'

'I know what to do, Mr Tarrant!' she retorted. 'If I didn't I should not be sitting here, should I?'

'Nor would you be sitting there if I myself were able to pilot this aircraft——' Clive stopped, interrupted by the pettish, complaining voice of his girl-friend, who, having come to the door, was asking what was going on.

'Can't you keep this thing steady?' she added, glaring at the back of Faun's head. 'I've never had such a terrible flight!'

'The aircraft is steady,' snapped Faun. 'It might interest you to know that you've been brought safely out of a region of violent turbulence.'

'Have you put the power on?' from Clive impatiently. 'It's time we were climbing.'

'I'm just putting it on.' Her hand moved to the throttles and she pushed them forward, glancing at the instrument panel as she did so. When full power was made she set the aircraft into a climb and for several seconds everything appeared to be proceeding smoothly. But suddenly the aircraft swerved to the right as Number Two engine flamed out. Faun, her heart giving a great lurch, riveted her eyes to the instrument panel and watched all the instruments for Number Two engine die down.

Clive spoke before she could, saying that Number Two engine was lost.

'Lost!' cried Ingrid, what little colour she still had instantly draining from her face. 'What——'

'Be quiet!' ordered Faun, aware that the 'fire attention getter' had begun to flash, and that she must immediately take the necessary fire drill for that engine. Clive was standing stock still now, and so was Tommy. Faun displayed no fear, even though her heartbeats were like sledgehammers in her chest. Outwardly she was calm, efficient, acting with all the confidence and ability which Clive himself would have shown in a similar emergency.

'I now suspect that the lightning strike ruptured the fuel line of Number Two engine,' she said. The fault had not come to light during the handling check; it was the increased pressure put on for the climb that had weakened the pipe.

Clive was nodding in agreement.

'And fuel probably spilled on to the hot engine—hence the fire——'

'Fire!' screamed Ingrid, ready to faint. 'Is the aircraft on fire?' Without affording Clive or Faun the time to answer she went on, 'It's no wonder, Clive, that you're dead set against women pilots! This expensive machine, on fire—and what about us? We'll all die——'

'Miss Fullman,' broke in Faun brusquely, 'will you please return to your seat?'

Both Clive and Tommy shot Faun a glance, and she waited for some comment from the arrogant boss, but he was not given the opportunity to speak, as Ingrid began to make some further complaint, this time about the way in which Faun had spoken to her. Faun replied, with a dignified authority, reminding her that as captain of the aircraft she was in a position to order her to return to her seat in the passenger cabin.

'I shall *not* take orders from you! Clive, surely it's you who are in command here—it *must* be!'

'How little you know,' murmured Faun, then turned away in contempt. Clive was again appealed to by his girl-friend, but he said nothing, his eyes fixed so intently on the top of Faun's head that she found herself glancing up. He was regarding her with a sort of questioning interest ... a strange unfathomable interest. Her own eyes challenged, because she was expecting him to insist on taking over command—even though he knew full well that his action would be a contravention of the rules of the Civil Aviation Authority. His mouth was set, his jawline taut. It seemed that in this mood of inflexibility Faun's efforts at retaining her rights would be futile. Yet her eyes continued to challenge, and she uttered the one short word,

'Well?'

The silence was preserved for a brief spell. Tommy, having freed Malcolm, was waiting for Clive's help in getting the unconscious pilot into the passenger cabin. The steward maintained a rigid countenance, as if he were deciding that, things being what they were, it behoved him to sit on the fence until it was decided which of these two headstrong people would eventually take command.

'Ingrid,' murmured Clive, his eyes on the instrument panel to which Faun's whole attention had returned, 'please return to your seat.'

'But——'

'You're in the way here,' he cut in, and now his voice was razor-sharp. 'Go, I say!' For a second she seemed about to protest, but the look on his face told her plainly that any further argument would bring down some humiliation upon her head, and she turned away and stalked back into the passenger cabin.

For the next few minutes Clive and Tommy were busy manoeuvring the inert body of the pilot so that it could be taken through the door to the cabin beyond. Clive waited only to see Malcolm comfortably settled on his back before returning to the cockpit where he took possession of the left-hand seat—the place which was always occupied by the captain of an aircraft.

'The radio's not working,' he was curtly informed as he began tinkering with it. 'The lightning strike put it out of order.' Faun paused a moment, her eyes on the panel. 'The compasses tumbled too, but I've managed to put mine right.'

He looked at her with a mask-like expression. What was he thinking? Surely he must have some admiration for the way she was handling the machine. Even a man so male-opinionated as he could not but admit that she had done as well as any man could do. He said quietly,

'Good. And now I'll see if I can do something with the radio.'

She wanted to say, sarcastically, that his voice had lost some degree of its arrogance and that she surmised the reason was that they had an emergency on their hands, but she refrained, very sure that he would not be stuck for a scathing rejoinder to whatever she might say.

She said suddenly,

'We can't make Singapore,' and to her astonishment he offered no argument. 'I've decided to divert, making for Borneo and the airport at Sarawak.'

He continued to tinker with the radio, a thoughtful expression on his face, as if he were carefully assessing the value of what she intended doing. Then he said,

'It's a pity the southern airport's closed for renovation. However, we should be able to make the airport at Sarawak.'

At length the island of Borneo was there, an island of rivers and jungle and tropical rain-forest, an island where, not so very long ago, head-hunters freely roamed, savages who were at home in the jungle, who were inured to the punishing tropical heat. Faun was tensed, every nerve alert to what lay in the balance. Never had she expected to be confronted with a test like the one which now faced her, but here it was, and she felt sure that if she could only land this crippled machine safely at the airport, then Clive Tarrant would be man enough to relent, to revise his opinion of women pilots, and to give her a permanent job with his firm.

But fate was not with her, for suddenly, without the slightest warning, the second engine flamed out.

'Hell!' exclaimed Clive, for instead of the reassuring roar of the engine there was now nothing but the sound of wind rushing past the aircraft.

'I—I——' A terrible fear entered into Faun; it rose

58

in her throat, preventing speech. Was this the end? But no! The situation might be desperate, but it was not hopeless. She must get the aircraft on to the ground within seconds, though; that fact forced itself into her mind with such urgency that she immediately looked down, scanning the terrain and mentally assessing her chances of making a successful crash landing.

'We're in real trouble now!' Clive was obviously chafing at the series of mishaps that had overtaken them; she also knew that he chafed at his own helplessness. But there was no fear either in his voice or his expression. He too was looking down, on to the thick impenetrable jungle that lay below. 'We shall have to land in the trees.' Turning, he called to the steward. 'We're making a crash landing! Macolm—how is he——?'

'He's come round——'

'A crash landing!' shrieked Ingrid from the back. 'Oh, not with her in charge, Clive! She's done enough damage already! Are you going to let her kill us? Clive, can't *you* take control?'

'Ingrid,' he said softly, but through gritting teeth, 'keep quiet!'

'I'm going to die——'

'Be quiet!' he snarled, uncaring for her terror, portrayed by her trembling body and staring eyes. 'Get yourself strapped in for the crash landing! Tommy, sit Malcolm up and strap him in! Miss Sheridan—are you all right?'

'I'm not likely to faint,' she just could not resist saying. 'I'm not such a poor specimen as that.' Nevertheless, she was tensed, and her face had lost much of its colour. For her efforts were futile; the plane was gliding and as it rapidly lost height the dark unfathomable jungle rushed up to meet it.

'Landing among trees is so dangerous,' she began, then stopped. 'Look!'

About five miles away was a dry river bed and, by some unforeseen working of nature, one fairly long length of it was straight.

Clive had seen it too.

'If we could manage to make that ...?' Faun was talking to herself, oblivious of the man beside her now. She *must* make that river bed!

She had no power at all, and with the plane fast losing height it seemed that there was imminent danger of its crashing, but with steadfast courage she persevered, refusing to admit defeat. A crash landing was inevitable, but if it could be made along that river bed there was far less chance of injury to the passengers, and also of sustaining a major injury to the aircraft.

'Do you think you can make it?' No arrogance in the voice now, not a hint of authority even. Clive Tarrant was fully alert to the tremendous strain which was being put upon Faun, and it would not only be ungracious, but highly dangerous, for him to say anything to upset her at this time.

'I can only try.' She spoke softly, feeling very feminine in this moment of terrible uncertainty and danger. She felt sure that, were it possible, she would gladly have handed over control of the plane to the man sitting beside her.

'Yes,' she heard him say, 'you can only try.' No fear in his voice and she turned, swiftly, to watch his expression. He had a certain amount of faith in her ability to land this aircraft safely on the river bed.

She would never know how she managed it ... but somehow the miracle was performed and the landing made without injuring any passenger or damaging the aircraft. It was a bumpy landing, though, for the river bed was strewn with boulders.

She looked at the taut face of the owner of the plane, endeavouring to read what lay beneath that mask. It was impossible, so even now she had no idea whether or not she was to achieve her ambition and work for his airline. But it was only natural that a sense of victory filled her when presently they were all off the plane and standing on the river bank—all except Malcolm, that was, who had had to be assisted by Tommy and Clive and who was now lying on the bank, conscious but obviously very ill, his breathing heavy and his lips blue and swollen. Looking down at him, Faun wondered if he would survive the ordeal which in evitably must now face them all, stranded in the midst of dense jungle—part of it primary jungle with trees reaching to heights of a hundred and fifty to two hundred feet, their tops forming a dense carpet through which little light could penetrate. The secondary jungle lay for the most part along the river bank, the dry part of the river being a wind-gap, Faun realised, the headwaters having been 'captured' by another river. In the region of secondary jungle the ground was covered by dense undergrowth and creepers, with an abundance of lianas clinging to the trunks of the trees, climbing in their search for sunlight.

'There's no risk of fire,' Clive was saying, but added

that they would wait a while before entering the plane, just for safety's sake.

'Oh, what are we to do?' cried Ingrid, glaring at Faun almost venomously. 'You could have killed us all!'

Tommy jerked, and opened his mouth to voice a strong protest, but closed it again, returning his attention to the sick man lying on the ground. Faun glanced at the girl for a mere second, contempt written all over her face.

'What are we going to do?' demanded Ingrid again, looking wildly about her and giving a shudder. 'We'll all be killed by wild animals!'

Faun's eyes glinted. She was fully aware that although Clive's attention was concentrated on Malcolm, he was at the same time listening to these hysterical utterings of his girl-friend.

'The best thing you can do,' Faun said to Ingrid, 'is resign yourself to this situation which we're all in. We shall need your help——'

'What sort of help?' broke in the girl rudely. 'If you think I'm going to play at Girl Guides and start rubbing sticks together then you're mistaken!'

In spite of herself Faun had to laugh, but she did it quietly, to herself, flashing a glance at Clive Tarrant. He saw the twinkle in her eyes and a very strange expression entered his.

'If you feel that way,' said Faun, 'then sit down and be quiet. Complaints won't help anyone.'

'You haven't answered my question! What are we going to do?'

Clive straightened up, and turned slowly to face her.

'Sit down,' he said quietly, then looked at Faun. 'You and Tommy can help me to bring out the dinghies; we need the supplies contained in them. We'll have to find something to catch the spilling fuel in——'

'Mr Tarrant,' broke in Faun gently, deciding that if she was to make a stand at all then she must make it now, otherwise the pompous Clive Tarrant was going to take over full command, 'I think you will agree that it's I who have the authority to give the orders?'

Silence, with both Tommy and Ingrid becoming tensely erect as they awaited Clive's answer. His dark eyes glinted; his mouth was set in a tight, inexorable line.

'I, as the owner of this aircraft, am in command.'

'I, as pilot of the aircraft, am the captain.'

Another silence. Faun wondered if she was wasting her time trying to establish her rights with a man so masterful as the boss of Tarrant Line. He was a man of strength, a man who was used to giving orders. She had told him, earlier, that she would love to have him in her power for a few minutes; she had the opportunity of having him in her power until they managed to extricate themselves from this precarious situation, but would he respect the rules and submit to her authority? It was very doubtful, but she was not surrendering without a fight, as he could see by the look in her eyes.

'Tommy,' he said at last, 'it's safe to enter the aircraft now. Find something to catch that spilling fuel; we'll need it when we light fires.' He looked straight at Faun. 'This matter's urgent. That fuel could save our lives. You fully understand this, of course.' A statement, because what he said was known to every aircraft crew. Fires must be lighted, in order to attract attention to themselves.

'The matter is urgent,' she agreed.

'In that case, we'll not go into any arguments as to who tells Tommy to find the containers.'

Faun glanced at Tommy; he moved towards the aircraft, refusing to meet her gaze. Ingrid was smirking, and she spoke, as if she just could not hold her tongue.

'Well, I'm glad that's settled, Clive, and you've shown this young woman just what her position is.'

Faun looked squarely at Clive.

'It is not settled, as your girl-friend maintains. For the present, because it's an emergency, I'm willing to hold my peace, but ...' Here she paused, to allow her next words to sink in. 'Later, Mr Tarrant, you and I shall be at war.' And with this she turned and followed Tommy, entering the aircraft in his wake.

CHAPTER FOUR

THE three of them worked hard to take from the aircraft all that was necessary for their immediate use.
Faun was elated that the machine was undamaged.
There had at first been a risk of fire, which meant that
the occupants had to leave the plane immediately it
had landed.

'Take a water container with you,' Faun had
ordered as she saw Ingrid rushing from the plane.
Water was vital to any survival and although Faun
knew that this terrain was one where they would have
heavy rain, she wanted the water taking off the plane.
But Ingrid was gone through the door, having ignored
the order given her by Faun. Clive and Tommy had
been urgently occupied with getting Malcolm off, and
it was left to Faun to pick up two heavy containers and
carry them with her as she left the aircraft. Faun had
then given the girl another order.

'Get upwind!' she cried, seeing Ingrid going in the
wrong direction. The girl took no notice and Faun repeated the order, putting it more plainly. 'Come this
way, at once!' Again she was ignored. Clive called to
the girl in a rasping voice,

'Get upwind! If the plane bursts into flames you'll
be enveloped in them!'

At this Ingrid wheeled around and raced back to
join Faun, who was running with the heavy water containers. Faun went back for another two, boarding the

plane as soon as the two men had got the sick man off. After that they all stayed away from the aircraft, three of them watching anxiously for any sign that it was going to burst into flames. They knew that if it did then many valuable commodities would be lost, items which would help both in their safety and their comfort. However, it was eventually seen that there would be no fire, much to their relief. Ingrid, continually glancing around, rather in the manner of some defenceless wild creature fearing the attack of a predator, knew nothing of the deep anxiety which her companions were undergoing. She kept muttering things like,

'We'll die of starvation ... we'll be eaten alive by lions and tigers ... we'll be savaged by apes!'

'There aren't any lions and tigers,' Faun said with contempt. The girl's general knowledge must be nil, she thought, again wondering what the boss of Tarrant Line could see in her. Beautiful but dumb had never been more appropriate!

'There,' Faun heard Clive say when at length the petrol had been saved, 'that will do for now.' He glanced at the items which had been brought from the plane. 'The first thing is for us to build a shelter, of course.'

'A shelter?' Ingrid, who had been standing by, watching the operations, gave a shudder and asked, 'Are we to live in log huts?'

Faun took a deep breath, telling herself that there was nothing to be gained by increasing the antagonism already existing between her and Clive's girl-friend. Yet she did wonder just how long she could tolerate the girl's stupidity, and her idleness. In a situation like this—and especially with a sick man on their hands— it was incumbent on everyone to pull their weight, but as things were it would appear that they had a parasite on their hands.

'Tommy,' Clive was saying, 'have you done all you can for Malcolm?'

Tommy nodded. He had brought out the first-aid box immediately on Faun's landing the aircraft, then dashed back to help Clive with the captain.

'He's comfortable,' said Tommy. 'A heart attack isn't something one can do much about.'

Clive shook his head, glancing with extreme impatience at the plaster in which his arm was encased.

'A most unfortunate occurrence.'

'If it hadn't happened,' put in Ingrid complainingly, 'we wouldn't all be in this terrible mess, for Malcolm would never have got the plane on fire and then crashed it in this dreadful jungle!'

Tommy, glancing from Ingrid to Faun, seemed to swallow something hard and nasty in his throat. But he made no comment, much to Faun's relief. She did not want any dissension to arise between the steward and his boss's girl-friend. A rescue would eventually be made, and it might go hard for Tommy if Clive had come to dislike him. Transferring her attention to Clive, Faun saw only an inscrutable expression on his bronzed face, yet she somehow felt sure that he was more than a little disgusted at the way Ingrid was conducting herself.

'We'll provide shelter for Malcolm first,' he said abruptly. 'Then we'll make ours. The two women will sleep in the aircraft.' He glanced indifferently from one to the other. 'I hope it won't be too much of a trial for either of you,' he added with an unexpected hint of humour.

Faun fixed his gaze a moment later and said, in firm emphatic tones,

'Mr Tarrant, I am the captain and therefore in charge of this situation. It's my orders that should be obeyed.'

He looked at down at her, his thin mouth curved in a half-sneer.

'The Amazon speaks again, eh? Take my advice, Miss Sheridan, and retreat, as if you don't you'll suffer a great deal of humiliation.'

'You're contravening the law of the air.'

'The aircraft belongs to me.'

Faun continued to fix his stare. She thought of the way she had brought them all to safety ... and there seemed to be only Tommy who had appreciated this. Well, that was not important; what was important to Faun was the upholding of her rights. Yet deep down within her she knew that she would be acting quite differently were it any other man standing here. She wanted Clive Tarrant to be in her power!—wanted to give him orders, and make him obey them! His arrogance and male egotism inflamed her and it was only natural that she should want to retaliate, to reduce him to a much lower level. But the man had more strength of character than anyone she had ever met; it was going to be exceedingly difficult to hold out against his dictatorial attitude. Faun decided to let her common sense prevail and wait until the time were more appropriate. For the present, Malcolm's comfort was the most important consideration, and the next was the making of shelters for the other two men.

Clive and Tommy began clearing away as much dead and rotting vegetation as possible, while Faun busied herself collecting dry twigs with which to make a fire. Ingrid, sitting on a fallen tree trunk, looked on sullenly for a few moments and then asked why the debris had to be cleared away.

'You could spread something over it,' she suggested.

'We clear it away,' said Tommy, 'because it'll be infested with ticks and ants, and probably leeches.'

'Leeches!' almost screamed Ingrid, jumping up and moving on to the dry river bed. 'Oh, if one should stick to me——'

'Perhaps,' interrupted Faun impatiently, 'you would help me to collect these twigs. I shall need a great deal.'

'What do you want to light a fire for?' demanded the girl. 'You've a butane stove; I saw Tommy bring it from the aeroplane.'

'A fire makes smoke,' replied Faun. 'And smoke keeps away the insects.'

'Insects ...' Ingrid's voice was now low, but a little cracked—with fright, thought Faun, casting her a disdainful glance. 'Do—do th-they sting?'

'Of course they sting,' answered Faun heartlessly.

Clive straightened up and looked at her. She met his gaze haughtily ... and yet he in turn showed no arrogance at all. His expression was strange, appearing to be a mixture of censure and amusement. So he didn't care for her attitude towards his lady-love, but at the same time it afforded him some kind of diversion!

Faun returned to her task, resigned to the fact that she would receive no assistance from Ingrid.

'You'll have to find a dry and sheltered spot before you light a fire,' warned Clive, and instantly received the retort,

'I believe I know the rules, Mr Tarrant!'

He glowered at her before turning away.

Faun found the sheltered place, under a leaning tree. She put down some dry grass and leaves, set these alight before adding a quantity of bark she had managed to take from a tree. Dead twigs came next and soon the fire was sending out smoke in huge clouds.

'You'll set the whole jungle on fire,' complained Ingrid from her place on a boulder in the river bed. 'Have you no sense?'

'Miss Sheridan has chosen a place where the fire can't spread,' Tommy told her. Faun smiled at him, aware that he was endeavouring to prevent her from uttering some scathing rejoinder to Ingrid's words. 'Air-crews have lectures on all these things.'

Ingrid turned away, found another boulder which was flat-topped, and sat down.

'Blast this arm!' Clive burst out suddenly. 'I'm not much help to you, Tommy.'

'That's all right,' returned the steward affably. 'Job's almost done.' He meant the clearing of the ground, of course, the erection of the shelter for Malcolm coming next. It was early afternoon, but nightfall was only four hours away, so there was an urgency about the two men, and in fact about Faun too. her self-appointed task being to make a bed for the sick man. For this she used one of the parachutes, folding it to the correct

70

size and then inserting dried leaves and grasses between the folds. A reasonably comfortable bed was produced, which was then placed in the shelter, this latter being made of supporting branches covered with part of another parachute, so that a tent-like shelter was created. Tommy and Clive managed to move Malcolm, who though trying to be brave did groan with pain now and then. Faun, now engaged on making a meal for them all, wondered again if the captain would be able to survive this ordeal. At present the air was cool, but tomorrow when the sun was at its fiercest there would be a most trying time for a man confined to his bed.

Faun used the butane stove to heat up tinned meat and vegetables—emergency rations which were always carried, even though it would be a hundred to one chance they would ever be used. She warmed up a tin of rice pudding which Ingrid condescended to carry in to Malcolm, after Faun had put it into a dish.

'He managed to take it,' Clive was saying with satisfaction when a short while later he emerged from the 'tent' in which the sick man lay. 'Have you a drink for him, Miss Sheridan?'

She nodded, indicating a flask which she had earlier brought from the aircraft.

'I've made some tea; it's in there keeping hot.'

Clive poured some of the tea into a cup and took it over to the tent. Faun was portioning out the meat and vegetables on to four plates. Ingrid eyed the food with disgust. She glanced around, making sure that she and Faun were alone. Tommy had gone to find a suitable place to establish sanitary arrangements and had not yet returned.

'What an unappetising mess! Do you expect any of us to eat that?'

Faun shrugged and casually said she could please herself.

'You're not at the Dorchester,' she just had to add, her eyes flickering over the girl disparagingly.

'You're insolent! You ought to be hanging your head in shame for what you've done! Crashing a beautiful aircraft like that—and nearly killing us all into the bargain. It must have been your incompetence that caused that fire.' Ingrid paused to see if Faun would speak. 'You've nothing to say, have you?'

'It wasn't the fire that caused us to make a crash landing.'

'It was the failure of the second engine—I'm aware of that. But to know the plane was on fire was nerve-racking, and to think it could all have been avoided——'

'Yes, it could,' broke in Faun, pale with anger, 'if only that dictatorial boy-friend of yours had listened to reason. I warned him that the weather was liable to prove a danger to flying, but he wouldn't heed me. Even when we were fully airborne he knew I wanted to return to Bali, but again he took no notice, either of me or of Malcolm.'

'You're blaming Clive for what's happened?'

'Not altogether; when something like this happens it's usually due to a combination of circumstances.'

'You *are* blaming Clive, so don't try to deny it. I shall tell him!'

Faun shrugged her shoulders.

'Do so by all means,' she encouraged, much to Ingrid's surprise. 'And you'll add a little something on, I shouldn't wonder.'

Tommy returned with the information that he had found just the place.

'I'll put up a sort of screen,' he promised, then added with a laugh, 'It won't be anything like the powder-room at the Bali Beach, but practical for all that.'

Faun responded to his laughter, while Ingrid shuddered visibly. Exchanging glances, Faun and the steward silently conveyed to each other their dislike of the girl.

'The meal's ready, I see,' from Clive on his return. 'Not what we've been having lately,' he said to Ingrid, 'but very welcome at a time like this.'

Faun's eyes moved swiftly, meeting his. Was he thanking her? She didn't want his thanks, and she let him see this by the expression in her eyes. She saw his own eyes glint and her lips twitched. How easy it was to rile the despicable creature!

'I don't think I can face it,' complained Ingrid. 'It looks quite nice, but I'm not hungry.'

'Looks nice?' from Faun, almost choking over the food in her mouth. 'But you just said——'

'If you will excuse me——' Ingrid glanced around, embracing them all, 'I'll go and rest in the plane.'

'Off you go, then,' returned Clive. 'I'll come and see you later.'

When the meal was over Clive became brisk and—to Faun's thinking—far too officious.

'Now that we've seen to Malcolm, and eaten, I want you to check the emergency rations, and list them. We can't be expected to be rescued yet awhile, so we shall have to go steady with the provisions, supplementing them with what this jungle can give us.'

As he turned abruptly, and as she knew there was no time to spare if he and Clive were to build two more shelters, Faun once again submitted to Clive's authority, although her blood boiled at the idea of having to obey his curtly-spoken orders.

The provisions—or most of them—were still inside the aircraft. Faun boarded, to see Ingrid sitting upright in one of the luxuriously-upholstered seats, her hands clasped tightly in front of her.

'I don't want to share this plane with you,' she blurted out before Faun could utter a word. 'We don't get on, so I think you should find somewhere else to sleep.'

'Nothing doing,' retorted Faun. 'There's room and enough in here. However, if your aversion's so great you yourself could find somewhere else to sleep. Go and ask your boy-friend to build you a shelter.'

'I think I will.'

Faun's eyes widened.

'You're not afraid of sleeping in a tent?'

The girl made no answer, but watched Faun instead as she made an inventory of the provisions.

'What's all this for?' asked Ingrid at last.

Faun explained, amazed that she could be civil; it struck her later that she was unconsciously realising that animosity would not serve in this present emergency. Morale was one of the most vitally important things, and Faun did not want Ingrid to become morose.

'We shall be here, in this jungle some time,' she warned. 'So we'll have to be very sparing with the food.'

'Surely we'll be rescued before very long?'

'We're expected at Singapore and when we don't arrive they'll send out a search rescue team, but as we've landed here, in this dense jungle, it's more likely we'll be here for a fair length of time before we're found.' Faun paused, wondering how much the girl could take. She felt she must have the stark facts put before her, yet at the same time she had no wish to frighten her. However, she did tell her that the radio was out of order and that Clive could do nothing with it. 'He might be able to repair it later,' she added hopefully, 'when he has the time.'

'What shall we do if the food runs out?'

'Go back to nature and eat what the jungle provides.'

Ingrid's eyes opened wide.

'Eat—grubs—and th-things?'

'I don't think it will come to that,' replied Faun calmly. She could have said that they might in the end be compelled to eat small reptiles such as frogs and lizards, but did not see any profit in putting the girl in possession of this fact. 'There's usually plenty of wild fruit to be found in a place like this.'

Ingrid frowned but fell silent, and Faun left her sitting there, staring into space.

It was dark when Faun, sitting by the fire she had

75

lighted and kept going, saw Clive go over to the air-craft. Tommy had gone to his shelter, declaring he was too tired to hold up, and in any case, there was nothing one could do once the daylight had gone. It had gone swiftly, as it always did in this part of the world, almost on the Equator. Faun had been able to appreci-ate the sunset in spite of everything. The fiery sphere had dropped and left behind a sky brilliant with every colour from flaming crimson to pale mauve. Fan-tastic cloud formations had held her attention, hover-ing as they did above the watershed. Clive had come to stand beside her, much to her surprise, and had said in an expressionless voice,

'Spectacular, isn't it?'

Faun nodded.

'Very. I've seen sunsets in many parts of the world, but none quite like this.'

Clive glanced skywards.

'Neither have I, come to think of it.'

Faun said,

'I've done the inventory. We shall have to adhere to strict rationing.'

'Obviously. No one will touch anything without my permission.'

'So you're determined to rob me of my authority?'

'With all your qualifications, Miss Sheridan, I'm amazed you missed one small point regarding the rules concerning a situation such as this.'

She frowned in puzzlement.

'I've attended the lectures. They're compulsory for all aircrews, as you very well know.'

76

'Yet you don't know that you're wrong in trying to assume command here?'

'I'm the captain, now that Malcolm's indisposed.'

'In the lectures which we give to our aircrews, we say that a leader must be elected——'

'That leader is the captain,' Faun could not help putting in knowledgeably, but to her surprise Clive was shaking his head.

'Let us have it correct, shall we?' he said, looking at her with a steely intentness. 'The leader is *usually* the captain. But in special circumstances another member of the crew may be better suited.'

'But you, Mr Tarrant,' pointed out Faun sweetly, 'are not a member of the crew.'

'Don't let's split hairs,' he snapped. 'However, if you would prefer that we elect a leader by vote, then I'm more than willing to oblige you.'

Faun had looked at him, seeing the ruthless lines of his face, the thin inflexible mouth. He was master of the situation and knew it.

'It would appear that I'm defeated,' she admitted, though with angry reluctance. 'Obviously the other three would vote for you.' He had merely nodded in a gesture of triumph, but even now, as she sat by the fire thinking about it, Faun felt a rise of fury that threatened to consume her.

Her thoughts were brought to an end by the appearance of the man himself; he had been in the aircraft with Ingrid for no more than ten minutes. He strode over to her and when he spoke his voice vibrated with anger.

'Did you tell Ingrid that I was to blame for the crash landing?'

'She repeated it? Oh, well, I told her to, seeing that she threatened she would. However, I didn't put all the blame on you——'

'Thanks,' he snapped. 'I'm greatly obliged to you, Miss Sheridan!'

'Don't mention it, Mr Tarrant.'

His eyes glinted like chipped ice.

'By God, girl, you'll see the worst side of me before very long!'

Faun opened her eyes wide.

'I haven't seen it already? How alarming, Mr Tarrant. I'm actually quaking with fear!'

'You'll be smarting with pain if you're not careful,' he threatened. 'Nothing would afford me greater satisfaction than to give you a clip over the ear!'

'You might get one back,' she said warningly.

'You're exceedingly brave, Miss Sheridan.'

'Amazons usually are. You forget they were fearless warriors.' She could not keep the amusement from her voice, and in the light from the fire she thought she saw his lips quiver. Was he too amused ... or was it fury that caused the gesture?

'You also told Ingrid that she ought to sleep somewhere else, that you preferred the aircraft all to yourself.' Clive spoke after a small pause and Faun gave a little gasp.

'It wasn't quite like that,' she returned. 'However, I'm not intending to vindicate myself, Mr Tarrant. If your girl-friend says I wanted the plane to myself, then you're at liberty to believe her.'

'Some people,' said Clive softly, 'would refer to you as a cat.'

She only laughed and flung back at him,

'And to you as a pompous, self-opinionated ass!'

Silence. Faun looked at him in the firelight. Forbidding, no doubt about that. So tall, his silhouette outlined against a background of dense jungle vegetation. Night sounds could be heard, those mysterious echoing noises that come from out of the primeval darkness. This was the deep *ulu*, the land of head-hunting tribes like the savage Ibans who had once made great sport of collecting skulls, the land of impenetrable undergrowth, of mango swamps and numberless rivers and their affluents.

'It would seem,' said Clive at last, 'that you and I are to be enemies, Miss Sheridan.'

She thought of how she had brought them safely down when both engines had been lost, and she had wondered if Clive Tarrant's opinion of women pilots had changed as a result. But he had not shown one degree of appreciation or friendliness and Faun was now resigned to the fact that she would never be employed by his firm. She had nothing to lose in consequence and this meant that she could speak her mind just whenever she chose.

'We could hardly be anything else,' she agreed, 'your opinion of my sex being what it is.'

His glance somehow strayed to the aircraft.

'All women are not like you,' he said.

'Nor like your lady-love,' she returned crisply. And could not resist adding, 'Thank goodness!'

The thin mouth went tight.

'We'll leave Ingrid out of it, if you don't mind?'

Faun said nothing; she had earlier found a flat piece of wood which she now used as a shovel on which she collected ash. But before she had time to do anything with it Clive was speaking again, surprising her by saying,

'You were intending to spread this around Malcolm's tent? I came to do just that.' He took the shovel of ash from her and she watched him stride away towards the shelter in which Malcolm lay. The ash would prevent the intrusion of the innumerable crawling insects which would otherwise have troubled the sick man. Clive came back for more, several times. 'I think I've covered the whole circle,' he said, throwing down the piece of wood. 'It's difficult to see even with the aid of the torch.' He stood looking down at her for a moment.

'Aren't you turning in yet?'

'I thought I'd keep the fire going for a while. You never know, we might attract the attention of some passing aircraft.'

'You're too optimistic. There won't be any aircraft flying over here. We can't expect anything in the way of a rescue yet awhile.'

'We'll have been missed by now.' Faun had thought about her parents many times since the forced landing; she thought about them again, deeply troubled by the anxiety that would soon be theirs.

'Just about,' said Clive. 'But as we've landed in this no-man's-land the search is likely to take some time. If I can get the radio working it'll be different, but I haven't much hope.'

'We can't make permanent camp here,' said Faun with a frown. 'There are swamps all around.'

'So you too have been surveying the land?'

She nodded and said in surprise,

'I didn't know you'd been looking around too.'

'I haven't. Tommy told me how unsuitable this place was, and thought we shouldn't stay here.'

'We couldn't have done anything else, though, at first, with being pushed for time as we were.' Faun realised, not without a high degree of surprise, that she and Clive were speaking to one another without any sign of hostility. A miracle! But how long would it last?

He said, as if reading her thoughts,

'If we're to be here for any length of time we might eventually bury the hatchet.' He seemed faintly amused by the start of disbelief she gave.

'I can't foresee anything more improbable,' she could not help retorting, but added, 'However, one never knows, Mr Tarrant. We might become so weak for the want of food that we haven't the strength to do combat with one another.'

Clive surprised her even yet again, by giving a gust of laughter.

'The Amazon has a sense of humour,' he said and, bidding her goodnight, he strode away in the direction of his shelter. Faun watched his figure, reluctantly admitting that there was something majestic about his carriage, a certain lithe and athletic spring to his walk. There was no denying his physical attractions; it was a pity the *inner man* was so abominable.

In spite of the way he and she were with one another, it was a surprise to Faun that he would go and leave her out here, in this jungle, which, like any other, would soon become alive with nocturnal creatures. Had she been in charge she would certainly not have retired and left Ingrid out here on her own. There was at least one dangerous animal in the jungle of Borneo, the honey bear, whose claws could easily kill.

Faun went slowly towards the plane, after putting out the fire by piling damp vegetation upon it. As she mounted the steps to the aircraft she turned. Clive Tarrant had come to the opening of his shelter and was watching her. So he had not really left her; he was alert, not going to bed until he had seen that she was safely inside the plane.

CHAPTER FIVE

THREE days had gone by and as yet there had been no sign of an aircraft overhead. Clive, after tinkering with the radio on and off for the first two days, was at last forced to admit that he would never get it to function.

'It's a pity,' Tommy said, 'especially as we've fixed our position from the topographical map.'

'Not our exact position,' corrected Clive, 'but near enough to have brought help had it been possible to send a radio message.' He glanced around automatically. 'We're somewhere near the confluence of the Mauri and Tarami Rivers—within five miles of it, perhaps.' They were all sitting in Malcolm's shelter, Malcolm himself propped up in his bed, some cushions from the aircraft having been brought into use for this purpose. 'I'm wondering if, at this confluence, there might be a Native longhouse.'

Ingrid's eyes dilated with fear.

'Do you mean a Native settlement?' she quavered.

'Yes, that's what I mean.'

Faun looked at the girl, contempt in her eyes. Clive, slanting a look at Faun, could not possibly fail to notice this expression, but Faun was not troubled. He should be aware of her opinion of Ingrid by now.

'Will—will th-they be head-hunters?'

'Probably,' answered Faun, forgetting, for the moment, her earlier resolve not to frighten the girl. Both Tommy and Malcolm laughed. Clive on the other hand glowered at Faun and seized the first opportunity of speaking to her about it.

'What are you trying to do to Ingrid?' he demanded. 'It isn't the first time you've tried to frighten her!'

In Faun's opinion the girl was a coward, but of course she kept this to herself. She did say, however, in tones of faint contempt,

'She's so scared of everything. I'd warned her to watch out for leeches and to examine her legs every few minutes. I also told her not to pull leeches off as they'd leave their jaws behind, but what does she do? Gives a scream and drags the leech off, with the result that she's now left with a festering sore on her ankle.'

Clive's hard eyes were expressionless; Faun wished she knew just what he himself thought about Ingrid.

'What you seem to forget,' he said, 'is that Ingrid has a very different personality from you.'

'She's feminine, you mean?' Faun's lips curved in a smile. 'I'm not, of course,' she added, watching for any change in his expression.

'You're correct on both counts, Miss Sheridan.' He paused. 'As you must have guessed, I prefer women to be feminine.'

'And that's why you like Ingrid. Well, if helplessness is anything to go by Miss Fullman's feminine enough for any man.'

'She is!'

Faun looked at him with a hint of humour in her eyes.

'How lucky can you get?' she retorted sarcastically. 'Will you marry her?' She knew the answer, but was astounded to hear him say quite frankly,

84

'I shall never marry anyone. I've more sense than to enter the kind of bondage that marriage represents.'

Her interest was caught and she found herself examining him in a new light.

'You sound as though you've already sampled that bondage,' she said at length, speaking slowly but with her senses alert. She saw the slight start he gave, noticed the merest hint of colour creep upwards at each side of his mouth. He turned his head abruptly. She heard him say in curt imperious tones,

'You'll stop trying to frighten Ingrid.' He turned again, his eyes glinting with the light of challenge. 'That's an order. Understand?'

Faun flushed.

'I'm not under your orders,' she snapped.

'Don't try my patience too far,' he advised. 'I've had just about enough of you!'

Faun opened her mouth to make a retort but closed it again, her attention arrested by the piercing *wak-wak-wak* of a gibbon's cry from somewhere in the dense undergrowth. Clive heard it too and was listening. Faun had discovered that she and this man had at least one thing in common: they were both interested in nature, in the flora and fauna of this primitive jungle in which they were being forced to live.

'I actually saw a gibbon yesterday.' Faun spoke softly, as though afraid of disturbing the ape even while aware that it was not close. She forgot her dislike of Clive for the moment, a smile appearing as she added, 'I'm hoping to see an orang-utan, though I know there are not many left now in their wild state.'

'They're so vulnerably friendly and tame. It's too

easy to capture them and put them into zoos.'

Faun nodded and a frown touched her brow.

'They're protected now, so their plight will not be so perilous.' She spoke seriously, her eyes a little brooding and faintly sad. Clive, his attention caught, was looking at her with an odd expression. He seemed different, somehow—not quite so arrogant and forbidding either in his appearance or his manner.

However, he made no comment on what she had said, and soon she was alone, watching his tall figure as he sauntered away towards the shelter in which Malcolm was resting.

With a faint sigh Faun wandered along the river bank, musing on several things as they flitted through her mind. She thought of her parents and sister; they would be almost out of their minds with worry, imagining all sorts of disasters that could have befallen the occupants of the luxury aircraft which had gone out to Bali to pick up her new employer. The firm would be unable to supply any information to any of the relatives of the crew, and the staff themselves must be going through a most anxious time. However, search parties would be out and sooner or later they would be over this jungle. They would be alerted by the fires which were already prepared, with cans of petrol standing close. Tommy and Clive were taking turns to stay up all night, in readiness to set the fires alight should they hear an aircraft anywhere within the vicinity.

At length Faun turned, retracing her steps. She glanced up, to the little plateau on a small rise where they had made their new camp. It was drier than the area they had occupied at first. Shelters had been made of bamboo framework with palm roofs, which meant that nothing from the plane had had to be used. The parachute canopies were draped over the trees and could be seen from the air; a huge sheet of tinfoil had also been utilised in a similar manner, but this was spread on the ground. It glittered in the sun and would be picked out at once if an aircraft should happen to be flying overhead.

Clive had allocated tasks. Faun's was the cooking, which at first was nothing more than warming up tinned food. However, Clive soon decided they must supplement their rations with what they could find around them. He sent Ingrid off to look for wild fruit; she went only after much grumbling and protesting. After the incident of the leech she refused to move far from the camp and in fact spent most of her time in the aircraft, playing patience or reading the glossy magazines which the airline always provided in quantity. She was bored; she complained of everything, not least of which was the food. She grumbled about not not being able to take a bath, whereupon Faun pointed out that Tommy had fixed up a shower, using one of the large water-containers which he attached to a rope. This rope was tied to a branch of a tree and the area around it was screened by bamboo poles draped with palm leaves.

'I'm not stripping off and getting under a bucket!' said Ingrid disgustedly. 'For one thing, what about the insects?'

Faun shrugged her shoulders, but Malcolm, having

recovered his sense of humour if not his full health, was unable to resist saying,

'Yes, indeed. You might be stung where it's difficult to fix a dressing!'

Ingrid glowered at him, while Tommy laughed outright. Clive wasn't present and so this mortifying experience suffered by his girl-friend was not witnessed by him. Faun had a strong suspicion, though, that it would not have occurred had Clive been there.

Becoming more and more irritated by Ingrid's complaints, Faun decided to let the girl have the exclusive use of the aircraft, as it was no fun lying there at night, being kept awake by Ingrid's pettish and fault-finding remarks.

'We'll have to ask Clive before we can build a shelter,' Tommy said when Faun asked for his assistance in constructing one of the palm and bamboo wigwam-like structures such as the men now had. 'Once we've got his permission we can begin.'

'Permission?' repeated Faun, and it was not until he noticed her expression that Tommy knew he had made a slip.

'Well ...' He looked apologetically at her. 'He told you to use the aircraft, and you can't change your plans without consulting the leader. It's all part of the rules, Faun. You know it as well as I do.'

Her mouth went tight.

'I'll make the shelter myself——'

'You'll never be able to cut that bamboo. It's tough.'

'There's a chopper we took from the aircraft. You and Clive used it with success.' She reflected for a moment on the way Clive had been able to help with the shelters. He had managed to use his right hand quite well and now he was scarcely affected by the plaster at all. He was tough and no mistake. He had no intention of allowing a thing like a Colles' fracture to put him out of action for long.

'You're supposed to use your hand,' had been his curt rejoinder when Tommy had warned him to take care. 'It does it good.'

'You can't wield that chopper!' exclaimed Tommy, quite appalled at the idea. But Faun merely let that pass, and went off to collect suitable lengths of bamboo.

Inevitably Clive saw her and demanded to know what she was about.

'It's time you were preparing the lunch,' he added before she could answer his question.

Faun returned tartly,

'Don't you think that Miss Fullman could do the lunch? I'm busy.' She looked up into his ruthless face, noting the thin-lipped mouth, the hard chiselled lines that spelled inflexibility. His blue eyes were unmoving, his voice very quiet as he asked again what she was doing.

'Building myself a shelter.'

Clive frowned at her.

'A shelter? What for?'

'To sleep in, of course.'

'You'll be far less comfortable than in the plane,' he warned her.

Faun shrugged this off.

'I prefer a place to myself.'

'Been having trouble with Ingrid?' he said perceptively. 'Just like women to get their priorities all wrong.'

He paused a moment; Faun recalled her discovery that he had been married and wondered if he had spoken to his wife in this aggravating way. 'You do realise,' he continued, 'that dissension is the greatest enemy of morale in a situation like this?'

'Are you putting the blame on me, Mr Tarrant?'

'You torment her; I've witnessed it.'

'Torment's a strong word.'

'I heard you tell her that the world's deadliest snake is to be found here, in this jungle.'

'Did you hear what went before I mentioned the snake?'

'I must admit I didn't.'

'Then don't judge until you know all the facts! Miss Fullman had asked me if there were snakes here; she was terrified of them, she said. I told her that snakes are usually just as eager to avoid humans as we are to avoid them. They usually glide away, as you know, and I told Miss Fullman so, but I did go on to warn her about the king cobra, which does sometimes attack without the slightest provocation.'

'I see.' Clive paused as if he had difficulty in finding the right words. Eventually Faun heard him say, 'I owe you an apology, then.' That was all. It was easy to see that even this had proved of the greatest difficulty to him.

Faun again asked him if he were putting the blame for the dissension on her and to her surprise he answered,

'Not entirely.' The concession caused her to give a slight start, which in turn brought a glimmer of amusement to his eyes. 'I'm afraid I can't let you have a shelter, Miss Sheridan. You'll have to put up with the lack of privacy; it'll not be for ever.'

She hesitated, profoundly aware of this man's tremendous strength of character. Could she hope to succeed in a battle of wills? No harm in trying, she decided.

'I still consider myself as the captain of that aircraft down there, Mr Tarrant, and don't intend to adhere to any of your orders that conflict with my own wishes.' There, it was out, and she cared nothing for the glint of fury that lit his eyes.

'Nor do I intend to permit insubordination,' he rejoined imperiously. 'I'm quite capable of putting you under lock and key.'

Faun's eyes blazed.

'Then you'd be cleverer than I thought, Mr Tarrant! How, might I ask, do you propose to make me a prisoner?'

'By putting you in the aircraft and appointing Ingrid as your jailer. She'd enjoy that,' he could not resist adding as an afterthought.

She flung him a defiant glance.

'Try it,' she challenged. 'You seem to forget that I have a far stronger character than this girl-friend of yours!'

'Forget?' with a lift of his brows. 'No one could ever forget your Amazon-like personality. It's in evidence all the time.'

'In that case, why don't you give up, and leave me alone?'

'Because,' he answered with an odd expression, 'you're a challenge to me, Miss Sheridan.'

'In other words, you've never met anyone who's had the courage to stand up to your tyranny?'

'Tyranny!' He gave a jerk of anger. 'I don't care for your choice of words!' he snapped.

'That's gratifying. I shall use more like that one.'

She really had roused his temper; it was evidenced by the drifts of crimson colour creeping slowly up the sides of his mouth, and by the compression of his lips.

'You're treading on dangerous ground,' he rasped. 'I advise you to have a care.'

The blue-green eyes challenged.

'And if I ignore your advice, Mr Tarrant?'

'You'll live to regret it.' He looked at her contemptuously. 'The trouble with you is that you're a poor loser. Just because I won't countenance your fraud and employ you, you're determined to do battle with me.'

'It may interest you to know,' she said quiveringly, 'that this is the first time I've ever been accused of being a poor loser! As for your not wanting to employ me—well, that's your affair. In any case, I wouldn't work for you now under any consideration!'

Clive merely shrugged his shoulders, appearing to be bored all at once. Faun said quietly that she was quite determined to have her own shelter, whether he liked it or not. To her astonishment he had no imperious answer ready. Instead, he gave her his full attention and she saw the sides of his mouth lift in amusement as he looked at her small hands—hands which, her father maintained, were exactly like her mother's—delicate and expressive, as a ballet-dancer's hands should be. Clive's glance was transferred to her body. He saw a slender frame with delectable curves and tiny waist. An

odd flickering in his eyes gave Faun the impression that
he was deciding he could pick her up with his one good
hand and toss her into the swamp without the slightest
trouble. To her amazement he shrugged his shoulders,
as if in a sort of amused decision, and said,

'You have my permission to build this shelter——'

'Permission!' cut in Faun, eyes blazing. 'I'm building it, Mr Tarrant, permission or no permission!'

He gritted his teeth, the hint of humour vanquished
by anger.

'Build it,' he told her in thundering tones, 'and cut
out the childish attitude of rebellion!'

Now why, Faun was asking herself as she watched
him stride wrathfully away, had he capitulated? There
was a very good reason for it; she had no doubt of that,
since such things as tolerance and understanding of her
position were the last considerations he would have had
in mind.

She left her task for the present; she had earlier
cut some tips and shoots of edible ferns, which she intended to boil as a vegetable. Bamboo shoots were also
on the menu and these, along with a tin of meat, formed
the first course, the second course being a fruit that
looked like an English chestnut but with the flavour of
the avocado pear. Faun had been delighted when,
having discovered the fruit growing on a tree, she had
tasted it—though with caution at first, remembering
that some fruits are poisonous—and found it so palatable. She was quite naturally pleased with all her finds
and the only difficulty she experienced was making
them look appetising on the plates. She took special
care over Malcolm's, whose appetite was by no means

good, although he was much improved in himself, being able to walk about a little. He had wanted to help with the erecting of the new shelters, but Clive insisted he take things easy.

'If you want to be helpful,' he said, 'then keep a log of what's happening. It'll make interesting reading one day, when this is just a memory.'

'You're very optimistic,' put in Ingrid, who was in one of her most fretful moods. 'Personally, I can't imagine our ever being found in this deep jungle. Oh, why did you allow Miss Sheridan to take over control of the plane!'

As Faun walked away in disgust she missed any reaction the men might have evidenced.

As she fully expected, Ingrid had some fault to find with the lunch. Earlier, the girl had scoffed at Faun's efforts only in the men's absence and Faun realised that Ingrid was play-acting in a way, slyly concealing her pettish complaints from Clive. Now, however, the girl did not seem to care whether or not she came down in his estimation.

'What on earth's this!' she exclaimed, picking up the green 'vegetable' with her fork and then letting it slip back on to her plate again. Faun coloured with anger and said tautly,

'Boiled fern—and consider yourself lucky you've got it!' She and the others were seated round the bamboo table. Faun had even been able to produce a cloth for it, using a gaily-coloured cotton headscarf she had brought with her and which was far larger than was either usual or necessary.

'It's quite tasty,' interposed Malcolm, trying to ease

94

the situation. 'What gave you the idea?' he asked Faun.

'I know that most ferns are edible, so it seemed a good idea to make use of them—although one wouldn't eat too much at first; it's a new food and could upset the digestion until one became used to it.'

'It would make *me* sick,' declared Ingrid, then she looked at Clive. 'Can't I have something else?' she pleaded.

He shook his head. Faun noticed that his eyes were narrowed and glinting as he replied,

'There's no reason why you should have anything different from what the rest of us are eating.'

The girl rose haughtily.

'In that case,' she snapped, 'I'll go without!'

Tommy and Malcolm were uncomfortable and Faun herself could have left the table. Clive seemed calm, and to be enjoying the meal.

'She could have eaten the meat, and the bamboo shoots,' said Malcolm. 'She must have had the shoots before.' No one said anything to this and Malcolm added, his eyes following the svelte figure of Ingrid as she went down to the aircraft, 'She'll starve to death if she goes on like this.' There was still no comment. Malcolm gave up and the meal was eaten in silence.

Faun spoke to Clive afterwards. She had wandered off, to search for suitable bamboo poles for her shelter, but had been sidetracked in her intention by sounds she heard coming from some trees that rose from among a dense thicket of tangled shrubs.

'What is it?' The quiet voice of the man she detested caused her to swing round.

'Tree frogs,' she answered curtly.

He came towards her, his eyes on her legs.

'Where are your slacks?' he demanded with a frown.

'Drying on the line I've improvised. I've washed them.' Her eyes automatically went to one of the water traps which Clive and Tommy had set up. There were many of these traps, quite simple in construction—just a large leaf suspended above a receptacle. In this way, rainwater, fresh and clear, was caught in plentiful quantities.

'You'll be stung,' Clive warned. 'And you've already got two leeches fastened to your calf.'

She frowned, and glanced down.

'What wretched creatures they are! It's said that every living thing has its use, but I fail to see what good these obnoxious attackers are.'

'Do you want my assistance,' he inquired with a sort of dry amusement, 'or are you fully prepared for this kind of eventuality?'

'I'm prepared,' she answered, drawing from her pocket a little bag she had made from one of her hand-kerchiefs. In the bag were several cigarette ends thrown away by Ingrid and which Faun picked up. She went to the water trap, took a quantity of water in her hand and dipped the bag into it, aware that Clive, watching her with interest, was nodding his head in a mechanical sort of way. Faun bent down and squeezed the nicotine on to one of the leeches; it dropped off and she treated the other one in a like manner.

'The super-efficient female.' Clive seemed quite unable to suppress this remark. 'It's to be hoped you never marry; you'd be a dead bore to your husband.'

Faun straightened up, angry colour filtering her cheeks.

'I want to speak to you about Miss Fullman,' she said tautly, deciding it was better not to voice the cutting riposte that had leapt to her lips. 'You spoke a short while back of dissension being the enemy of morale. You do realise, don't you, that your girl-friend deliberately makes herself objectionable to me? I don't know how much you're expecting me to take from her, but I should imagine that by now you know me well enough to be sure I'm coming to the end of my patience.' She paused, giving him an opportunity to say something, but he remained silent, watching her intently through his unmoving blue eyes. 'I naturally don't want to quarrel with her; she's intolerably bored already and a quarrel could further upset her. We don't want an hysterical woman on our hands, Mr Tarrant.'

Tight-lipped, he stared hard at her; there was something unfathomable about him, though his anger was evident. Whatever he himself thought about Ingrid, it certainly infuriated him to hear her spoken of disparagingly by another person. Well, thought Faun, at least he was to be admired for his loyalty. Admired? She frowned and looked him over. Apart from his physique, and his undeniably handsome looks, there was little else that could be admired. Still, she was willing to admit that he deserved a modicum of credit for his loyalty. He spoke at last, asking Faun if she could not be a little more understanding of Ingrid's character. His words, though edged with temper, were surprisingly quiet and Faun had the staggering impression that he actually felt some degree of admiration for her own cool efficiency.

'As you've said,' he continued before Faun could speak, 'we don't want Ingrid's morale to break——' Again he stopped, this time halted by the swift raising of Faun's eyebrows.

'You put it far more politely than I did, Mr Tarrant.'

'I detest the word hysterical,' he returned brusquely.

Faun shrugged.

'Very well, choose your own words. It isn't the first time you've made an objection to mine.'

'Do you have to start a damned argument every time you and I meet?' he demanded exasperatedly. 'For heaven's sake, woman, try to be a bit more amenable, for if you don't I won't be responsible for my actions!'

She looked at his hands, noting the tightly-clenched fists. His shirt sleeves were rolled up, despite the dangers of being stung by insects; she saw the strong light-brown hair that covered his arm, and her eyes went automatically to the other arm, encased in plaster right up to the elbow. She said, unable to resist it,

'That you'd like to do me an injury is obvious, Mr Tarrant.'

'I'd like to shake you till your teeth rattle!'

For some reason she had to laugh ... and to her amazement Clive Tarrant responded. And then there was silence, deep and profound, and a tenseness in the air that was beyond the power of words. Faun shifted her weight from one leg to another in a shuffling movement that seemed to bring a glimmer of satisfaction to those deep-set blue eyes of his. He believed her to be disconcerted, nervous, even. But she was not ... or was she? There was no denying the slight increase in her heartbeats, or that a strange sensation quivered within her, affecting her nerves in some way she failed to understand. Where was the fire that was so ready to be ignited whenever this man came into her presence? And what of Clive himself? Where was that arrogant sneer, that gleam of contempt that invariably lurked in his expression whenever he looked at her?

The silence was broken by a snapping sound that rent the air. A tree had fallen somewhere close at hand; it would merge with the reeking wetness of the ground beneath its dense covering of luxuriant vegetation where it would rot away like millions of other trees during the aeons of time in which this primordial jungle had flourished. The breaking of the silence came as a relief to Faun, affected as she was by this indefinable sensation that was both unfamiliar and faintly exciting.

'I expect the tree frogs have gone,' she said, deliberately avoiding the subject of Ingrid. 'I'm making a list of all the animals I've seen.'

'You are?' His eyes went past her to the place where the tree frogs had been. 'And what have you on this list?'

'Hornbills and a civet cat. Lizards, of course, as they are all over the place. I wish I knew the different kinds.'

'I believe they have about a hundred different kinds in Borneo.'

'So many? I didn't know that.'

'Have you seen the flying lizard yet?'

Faun shook her head.

'Does it really fly? I rather thought it merely glided.'

'As a matter of fact it does glide, on certain membranes.'

Faun nodded, then mentioned the birds' calls she had heard.

'I'm also making a list of the flowers I've come across,' she added. 'And the fruits, of course.'

'Have you discovered the durian yet?'

Faun shook her head.

'I've heard of it, though. It's an acquired taste, I believe?'

'Yes.' He glanced upstream casually. 'If we can find some we'll be able to use them as an alternative to the fruit you used at lunch time today.'

Faun said nothing; she was just begining to realise that this was almost a friendly conversation. The arrogant boss of the Tarrant Line was human for a change, revealing what could almost be an attractiveness beneath the veneer of haughty superiority. He spoke after a while, asking about the shelter she proposed building for herself.

'As a matter of fact I was just about to collect some bamboo poles when my attention was diverted by the tree frogs,' she told him.

'Don't let me detain you, then,' he said, and left her.

She stood for a long moment, her face set in thoughtful lines. She was aware of some kind of evasion within her as if she shirked an admission that would have aroused her anger. Her forehead puckered in a frown of annoyance as she tried unsuccessfully to overcome the evasion and analyse her feelings at this particular moment, as she stood here in this teeming humid jungle, moved in some unfathomable way by the fact that she

100

and Clive Tarrant had, for once, managed to converse in a manner verging on friendliness.

At last she gave a sigh of impatience and picked up the chopper from where she had left it when she heard the sound of the tree frogs close by.

CHAPTER SIX

THERE was a distinct thread of satire in Clive's voice as, returning back from the walk he had taken along the river bank, he asked Faun how she was getting on.

'Fine,' she answered, instantly putting one hand behind her back. With her right hand she was just going to chop at a length of bamboo cane when Clive said swiftly,

'Fine, eh? And why are you hiding——'

'Yes, fine,' interrupted Faun with a trace of defiance. 'I'm thoroughly enjoying it.' She winced as she spoke, but averted her head, hoping he had not noticed.

'You're finding it exhausting, though.' A statement, which afforded him extreme satisfaction, she thought. 'Don't you dare deny it,' he told her. 'I'm not such a fool that I can't see that you're just about all in. Wouldn't Tommy help you?' His eyes went to her side, the left side. Faun hoped that blood was not dripping from the wound she had just inflicted upon herself.

'I refused his help.' She reflected on Tommy's offer that he give her some assistance, once she had told him that Clive was in agreement with her having the shelter. She had refused his help simply because it occurred to her that Clive's only reason for that capitulation was the conviction that the task would prove beyond her. She was in consequence, determined to let him see he was mistaken.

'Refused his help?' repeated Clive with a hint of perception.

'I wanted the satisfaction of doing it myself.'

'Or of proving to me that you could do it yourself,' he rejoined levelly.

Being an honest person Faun had to own that his assumption was correct, at which he told her that she was far more transparent than she knew. She had nothing to say to this, having heard her father make the same pronouncement on many occasions.

'You mustn't waste your time here,' she said presently, wanting only to get to the first-aid box and find something to take the pain from her hand. 'I expect you've plenty to do.'

'What have you done to that hand?' The question was put imperiously and immediately followed by an order to bring her hand forward.

'It's nothing; I merely——' She got no further as, with an impatient exclamation, Clive snatched the chopper from her, tossed it on the ground, then took hold of her arm and swung her round.

'You wretch!' he murmured softly. Her hand was bleeding profusely and she actually gave a little cry when he began to probe beneath the blood to find the wound. 'So you're not as clever as you thought you were, eh?—not quite so tough as you'd like me to believe? I've a good mind to make you howl like that again——'

'I didn't howl!' she blazed. 'Leave go of my wrist!'

'If I do it'll be to put you across my knee and make you smart!'

'Oh ...!' Faun's fury prevented anything more than

that; she felt that a conflagration was consuming her whole body.

'Come on!' he commanded, but gave her no choice as he literally dragged her towards the spare shelter which served as a sort of communal sitting-room. In it were stored the tinned rations, the first-aid kit and several other items taken from the aircraft. 'Sit down, and don't you dare move while I'm away getting water!'

She found herself obeying him, rather to her chagrin, but the pain was becoming too uncomfortable for her to argue.

'There's some boiled water in one of the flasks,' she said.

'Where?'

Faun gestured to a bamboo table which stood in the corner, made by Tommy who jokingly said he would take up jungle craft for a living, he was becoming so good at it.

'On there.'

'Give me your hand,' he was saying a moment later as he stood over her, his height and his manner so over-powering that she wanted to get up and run from him. 'So, Miss Competent!—you don't know everything, apparently. You didn't realise you had to take the greatest care when working bamboo, did you?' Faun made no answer; she was in fact having to bite her lip hard in order to hold back the little cries of pain that rose convulsively in her throat. 'You never realised that the outer skin of bamboo, when split, could injure you like this!' He glowered down at her, his mouth tight. 'I ought to box your damned ears for your stubborn stupidity! This wound's deep; it could be dangerous!' He had finished bathing it, saying brusquely that he hoped it was cleansed of all dirt. 'We can only hope so,' he went on wrathfully. 'And now hold this pad while I get a bandage!'

She sat there meekly, wondering what was the matter with her that she was showing so little spirit. But the astounding truth was that she wanted to cry, so dreadful was the pain. And in fact she did feel a trace of moisture in her eyes and averted her head swiftly. Clive bandaged the wound and then, with an unexpected gesture of imperiousness, he put a hand under her chin and tilted up her head. His blue eyes were still, his mouth compressed.

'No use being sorry for yourself now; it's too late for that.'

'I'm not sorry for myself!'

'You will be before you're much older!'

The tears were more persistent and she swallowed, fighting against allowing this man to see her crying. How he would gloat! She would never be able to bear the humiliation.

'I think I'll go and lie down.'

'A good idea. In fact, I was just about to order you to.' He spoke with a taunting edge to his voice; Faun ignored his deliberate attempt to rile her and said, just as if she had not heard his words at all,

'Yes, it is a good idea, Mr Tarrant. Er—if I'm not about to get the evening meal ready there's some more bamboo shoots to use with the tinned fish.'

'Did I tell you to use the fish?'

'You said I could use two tins a day. We've had meat, so I thought the fish would be a change.'

'I rather think we shall have to reduce our ration to one tin per day.'

She gave a deep sigh.

'I wish we could get the radio working. It would solve all our problems.'

'I've had another try, but given up. It's impossible to do anything with it.'

Faun went to the aircraft to lie down. Ingrid was there, playing cards and smoking a cigarette. There had been a plentiful supply of cigarettes on the luxury aircraft and as Ingrid was the only one who smoked she was not likely to run out yet awhile. Faun, aware of her boredom and her irritability, hoped and prayed that the cigarettes would last out until the rescue party arrived.

'What's wrong with you?' Ingrid wanted to know, eyeing the bandage. 'Who's done that for you?' The arrogance in her tone matched the expression in her eyes and Faun could not help thinking of Clive and his own haughty manner of approaching people.

'I've gashed my hand on some bamboo skin.'

'Is it serious?'

Faun shook her head.

'No, I don't think so.'

A small silence and then,

'Who bandaged it for you?'

'Mr Tarrant.' Faun moved over to the reclining chair which served as her bed and sat down. She felt rather sick and weak and realised she had lost a good deal of blood while standing there, talking to Clive.

'Clive!' Ingrid spoke sharply, her eyes darkly frowning. 'I thought you and he were enemies.'

'Enmity's put aside in an emergency. I had no one else to dress the wound for me.'

'Tommy could have done it!'

'He wasn't there.' Faun had to smile; the girl was plainly annoyed at the idea of Clive dressing the wound for her.

'I could have done it, if you'd asked me.'

The remark provided the opening Faun had wanted for some time.

'I wouldn't have asked you, since you've proved so reluctant to do anything at all.'

Ingrid coloured, though her expression was one of brittle arrogance.

'You're impertinent, Miss Sheridan! You seem to forget your position!'

'My position?' repeated Faun, puzzled.

'You're nothing more than a—well—a servant, are you?'

Faun looked at her, her restraint almost broken by the girl's insolence. However, conscious of her morale being liable to collapse if her nerves became too frayed, Faun trod carefully, for as she had told Clive, they didn't want an hysterical woman on their hands at a time like this.

'The fact that I choose to make myself useful,' she said at length, 'doesn't mean that I'm a servant.'

'Clive considers you to be a servant; that's why he doesn't hesitate to order you about the way he does.'

Leaning back, Faun relaxed, telling herself not to lose her temper no matter how great the provocation. A quarrel would do neither of them any good, and it could do Ingrid a lot of harm.

'I'm intending to rest,' she told the girl. 'Please try to be quiet; I might manage to have a sleep.' She closed her eyes, wishing she had been more careful with that bamboo, for the pain was now a dull throb that increased her feeling of sickness. The cigarette smoke did not help; it was a dun-yellow pall which hurt Faun's eyes and throat.

'I don't see why I should have to be totally silent,' protested Ingrid sullenly. 'After all, this is my sleeping place as well as yours.'

Faun's eyes lit with anger, but again she decided it would be more prudent to ignore the bait. For bait it was; Faun saw this very clearly. Ingrid was going out of her way to pick a quarrel. It would ease her boredom, for the moment, but after that it would result in depression, though Ingrid was not aware of this.

'I'm merely asking that you don't talk to me,' said Faun mildly. 'The pain's pretty bad and it's making me feel off-colour.'

'Sick, you mean?'

'Yes, that's right.'

'How—revolting!' The girl paused. 'Are you just saying that so I'll get out of here and leave you on your own?'

'Certainly not,' answered Faun wearily. Would the girl never stop talking?

'I think you are! I shall go, but I'll mention your trick to Clive!'

'Mention it by all means,' said Faun exasperatedly, turning into the cushion that served as a pillow. Ingrid departed; Faun let the chair right down and flopped back. She hadn't the strength to unfold the blanket and spread it over her.

She awoke about an hour later, brought from her sleep by the perceptive instinct that she was no longer alone. Clive was standing over her, an odd expression in his eyes.

'Did I waken you?' he asked as if angry with himself.

'It doesn't matter.' Faun put up her hand to stifle a yawn. She felt slightly dazed and decided she was not yet properly awake. 'Did Miss Fullman come to you?'

A strange silence followed her question before Clive said, a hardness in his voice that had not been there when he first spoke,

'Why do you ask?'

'She said she would be telling you about my trick——' Faun broke off, fully awake now and regretting her slip.

'How are you feeling?' Clive's tone had lost that hardness already. 'The injury hurts?'

She nodded and tried to sit up. To her amazement she was assisted to a sitting position and the cushion propped up behind her. She looked down, her eyes widening.

'The blanket,' she murmured, 'you put it over me.' She glanced up into his bronzed face and a strange tremor passed through her. His nearness disturbed her, his attentiveness was disconcerting because it was so unexpected. He baffled her even by his presence here as she could see no reason why he should trouble himself about her. If she were laid up at least she would be out of his way.

'It wakened you, unfortunately. But you would have begun to feel very cold had you stayed here much longer without a cover. The sun's going down and you know how chilly the nights are.'

'It was—was kind of you, Mr Tarrant.' She felt shy all at once, and there was a constriction in her throat which she could not understand. Clive had straightened up after putting the cushion at her back and he made no attempt to break the silence as he stood there, surveying her critically. Her skin was pale, but with a bloom of delicate peach in her cheeks; her thickly-fringed eyes of translucent blue-green were widely-spaced beneath arched brows, her chestnut hair fell about her shoulders like a silken cloak. Never had she appeared more feminine, or vulnerable, although Faun herself was totally unaware of this. And when she saw Clive's brows come together in a frown she naturally put this down to impatience. He was still annoyed with her for wielding that chopper. She felt a sort of misery welling up inside her and before she quite knew it she had spoken her thoughts aloud.

'I feel so depressed.'

'Did you manage to be sick?' he asked matter-of-factly.

Faun shuddered, then said, her swift-winged thoughts going back to Ingrid,

'That was a trick——'

'I asked you a question,' snapped Clive. 'Answer me!'

She shook her head at once and said no, she had not been sick.

'I don't want to be, either,' she could not help adding.

'You'd have felt better if you had been. I'd give you a salt and water drink, but we can't spare the salt. What made you depressed?'

She glanced down at her bandaged hand which she had brought from beneath the blanket.

'Perhaps it's because I've done this. It makes me feel helpless.'

She saw his expression change as a quality of satire took the severity from his face.

'You'll regret that admission tomorrow, when you're more yourself.'

Was the man actually teasing her? If so, what on earth had brought about the dramatic change in his attitude towards her?

'I expect you're right,' was all she could find to say. She was thinking of his relationship with Ingrid, his indifference towards her since the crash landing. More than ever it seemed to Faun that there was no affection in the relationship, that Clive used the girl merely to while away the tedium of those interludes which would otherwise have been dull.

She looked up at him, expecting him to come out with some taunting rejoinder, but obviously he was not intending to do any such thing, for his face was relaxed into soft lines she had never seen before. This change mystified her, disturbed her senses in a way that both vexed and puzzled her. His sudden smile did nothing to restore her equanimity; just the reverse, since it was a *friendly* smile which gave her a new awareness of him as a man. Up till now he had been her enemy, a pompous arrogant male who believed that women had no place of importance now, any more than they had in the past. But suddenly he was not pompous and arrogant at all, but just a handsome man with a most charming smile upon his lips.

'I must be dreaming,' whispered Faun to herself. 'I'm not awake yet.'

'What are you thinking about?' he wanted to know,

his voice quiet and pleasingly modulated. 'Your lips were moving with your thoughts.'

'You're imagining things,' was her evasive reply, but Clive shook his head.

'You're a strange girl,' was his unexpected comment, and Faun glanced up quickly, into an inscrutable countenance. 'I said you are a challenge, and I meant it.'

'That,' she told him, 'is cryptic. I don't know what you mean?'

The deep-set eyes flickered over her face; that he was interested in her was plain, and his next words did not exactly come as a surprise to her.

'You're not a woman to be ignored, Miss Sheridan. But you don't need me to tell you that.'

'No,' she agreed frankly, then added that it was only because of her unusual occupation. 'People are always amazed when I mention my flying career.'

'That's understandable,' he returned with some amusement. 'You're not the size of six pennyworth of copper.'

Faun's eyes widened.

'You've changed, Mr Tarrant. To what do I owe this sudden friendliness?'

'I'm not being friendly, Miss Sheridan, but merely stating facts.' His glance shifted to her hand. 'The pain's still bad?'

'It throbs, but it'll go eventually.' She touched the bandage automatically. 'I wish I'd known about the bamboo!'

'You oughtn't to have decided to make yourself a shelter. There's nothing wrong with this place.'

Except that she was forced to share it with Ingrid,

Faun could have added, but she refrained because, for some incredible reason, she was reluctant to arouse his animosity again. She said, looking up into his bronzed face,

'I still want my own place to sleep, Mr Tarrant.'

He frowned, as she expected he would, and his mouth compressed into an inflexible line. Oh, dear, was he going to revert to that dictatorial attitude again? Faun felt she could not endure an argument just now. Her head was aching, though she would not have mentioned this for anything. When he had gone she would take a couple of aspirins, a supply of which had been left in the aircraft.

'We could be rescued in a day or two,' he said, 'and in view of this it would be a waste of time to build a shelter.'

'It doesn't take long; besides, it's something to do. I can't stand this inactivity.'

To her surprise he agreed that the inactivity was affecting him as well.

'It breeds boredom, and that's fatal in circumstances such as these.'

'Tommy's overcome the inactivity, hasn't he?'

Clive nodded and smiled.

'He's taken up jungle craft quite seriously. He's making a trap at present, with the idea of catching a wild pig.'

'Are there wild pigs in this country?'

Clive nodded.

'They used to be numerous at one time, and I believe they're still fairly plentiful. The Natives depend on them for protein—in addition to other foods, of course.'

'It would be a pleasant change to have some fresh meat, but I don't want to see a pig in a trap.' She shuddered visibly, bringing an odd expression to the man standing there, his height overpowering, his personality affecting her in the most disturbing way.

'One has to kill in circumstances such as we are in,' he told her, and now there was a gravity in his voice which she had not heard before. 'If we're not rescued in the next few days we'll be reduced to eating lizards, and perhaps snakes, if we can catch them.' He paused a moment as if waiting for some reaction, but Faun was silent, trying not to think about eating anything so revolting as a snake. She had already accepted that they might have to eat frogs, and even ants and grubs, but never had she anticipated using snakes as food. 'Also, I'm thinking of taking a trip up river, to the confluence I spoke of. There could be a longhouse thereabouts, as I said. If so we might get the help of a Native——'

'They might not be friendly,' Faun broke in, wondering why she felt so agitated at the idea of Clive's going to the longhouse alone. 'After all, it isn't such a long time since they were head-hunters, is it?'

'A fair time,' returned Clive casually. 'The Brookes did a great deal to put a stop to it.'

'But tradition dies hard,' Faun persisted. 'I wouldn't go if I were you, Mr Tarrant.' He was looking strangely at her, as if both puzzled and surprised by her anxiety.

'We'll see. I have a feeling, though, that we might have to look for help from some local source.'

Faun shivered.

'We're not desperate, Mr Tarrant—and if Tommy

can make these traps you speak of then we shall manage very well for food.'

Clive stared down at her, his regard disconcertingly intense.

'You're obviously not too perturbed by our situation, Miss Sheridan.' It was half statement, half question, but what could not possibly be missed by Faun was the quality of admiration in his tone. Whether or not he meant her to recognise it she could not have said; all she knew was that it was there, and that it gave her a little access of pleasure to know that his opinion of her was undergoing a change.

'As you say, Mr Tarrant, I'm not too perturbed. Don't imagine, though, that I'm ignorant of the seriousness of our plight. But I can't help remembering that we're lucky to be alive at all——' She stopped abruptly, fearing he might be secretly accusing her of boasting of that miraculous crash landing she had made. But to her astonishment he was nodding, and there was not the slightest hint of contempt in his voice as he murmured, almost to himself,

'Yes, indeed, we're lucky to be alive at all.'

Faun felt the colour rise to tint her cheeks, and she turned away so that her expression was shielded from those discerning eyes. What was happening to her that she felt so unsure of herself, so very feminine, so shy? The silence became too much for her, because it savoured of intimacy, of a closeness which was known only to comrades. And so she had to break the silence, and the only thing she could bring to mind was the shelter. She asked him if she could have it, unaware of the content of her words until she saw the broad smile

115

of amusement that leapt unexpectedly to Clive Tarrant's mouth. She had requested, not demanded.

'I *am* having it,' she instantly corrected. 'It was merely a slip of the tongue that I *asked* if I could have it.'

There was a defiance in her amended words, and a certain degree of hauteur, and yet, mingled with her candour, they had an appealing quality which—though she did not know it—had the most unusual effect on Clive.

All she did know was that, later, when she got up and went along to the place where the other shelters were, she observed a sight that staggered her. Clive, with the assistance of Tommy, was busily engaged in preparing bamboo poles of the appropriate length for a shelter. Ingrid was standing some small distance from the two men, and even though it was now growing dark, Faun could clearly see the twist of anger on the girl's lips. Faun moved away, unseen by any of them, and went back to the aircraft, having decided it was more prudent, at this particular time, to keep out of the way.

CHAPTER SEVEN

THE shelter was finished by the following afternoon and Faun, the pain in her hand having eased a little, moved her belongings from the plane to her new sleeping quarters. Tommy had already made her a small stool and on this she put the couple of books she had brought with her. Her suitcase she put on a little platform she had made herself from a box she had taken from the aircraft. Tommy was engaged in making her a bed out of interwoven palm leaves fastened to a framework of bamboo. The bed had four stout poles, one at each corner, which kept it off the ground and also extended about a foot above the palm mattress.

'If you've a negligée you're not using you can drape it over the top two poles and use it as a mosquito net,' Tommy suggested. 'You'll certainly need a net if you're sleeping outside.' Both he and Malcolm had naturally been puzzled by Faun's firm decision to build a shelter, but neither of them had said anything to her about it. Tommy, glancing up from his task of weaving the palm leaves together, saw that Faun was looking rather puzzled.

'How are you going to fix this mattress to the frame?' she wanted to know. She, like Malcolm and Clive, was intrigued by the way Tommy had developed this skill for working bamboo. That he had a flair for it was plain, and he himself expressed surprise at the quality

117

of his work. Already he had made the table and stools, and had begun to make a chair, which he had left in order to help with Faun's shelter and to make her the bed. For Malcolm he had made a sort of cabinet for the side of his bed, as Malcolm spent much of his time resting, mainly on the orders of Clive, who made no pretence of the fact that he did not want an invalid on his hands. Another attack could mean that Malcolm was confined to bed the whole time, and when the rescue party did arrive their task would be made more difficult by their having to deal with a stretcher of sorts, hauling it into the helicopter.

'I've no rope, you're thinking?' Tommy grinned at Faun and told her triumphantly that he had solved the problem of binding materials for his furniture-making. 'I'm using the fibre of climbing canes—you've no idea just how strong it is. Then there's the fibre of the lianas; that's quite strong too.'

Faun's gaze was appreciative and so was Clive's. Ingrid, sitting on one of the bamboo stools, merely looked on in silence. She was becoming more and more bored, having perused the magazines over and over again. If only she would try to find an interest, mused Faun, then she would not be nearly so bored as she was. Could she, Faun, persuade her to come on a nature walk with her? she wondered. It was worth a try, and the following morning Faun invited her to take a stroll with her along the river bank.

'I'm searching for the wild hibiscus which I believe grows here,' Faun said. 'Perhaps you could help me to find it?'

'I'm not wandering along that bank,' was Ingrid's

immediate answer. 'The vegetation's alive with leeches and ants.'

'You have to watch for them. In any case, you've some slacks you can wear. I tie mine up around the bottoms so that nothing can get into them.' Faun paused, but Ingrid remained sullenly silent. 'Nature's most interesting,' persevered Faun, 'as you'd soon find out if you came on these walks with me.'

'I've no wish to find out,' snapped Ingrid, 'not any more than I've any wish for your company. As for this interest in nature—well, it doesn't go with flying planes, that's for certain.'

'I don't see why you're making the comparison. One is my occupation and the other my hobby. Everyone should have a hobby, Miss Fullman. Look at Tommy; he's making a hobby of working bamboo, and he'll keep it up when he gets back home——'

'If he ever does get back home!' flashed Ingrid, her dark eyes baleful and accusing. 'You do realise, I suppose, that if we all die here, in this dreadful jungle, it'll be you who have murdered us?'

Faun looked at her in contempt, deciding it was no use wasting time trying to be pleasant to the girl. She was insulting and complaining in turn; with Clive she was now adopting a querulous attitude, and with the other two men her manner was one of indifference.

Faun went off on her own and to her delight she found what she was searching for. She sketched it in her notebook, adding various items of interest which included its environment. Clive came upon her as she returned; she was so busy reading what she had written that she would have bumped into him had he not

119

spoken a few seconds before they reached one another.

'You're very interested,' he observed, his eyes on the notebook. 'More discoveries, I take it?'

She nodded, smiling. It seemed months since she and Clive were at each other's throats.

'I've found a wild hibiscus!' she exclaimed, happier than she realised at speaking to someone who was just as keen as she and so would be interested in her discovery. 'It's very attractive, as you can see from my drawing—perhaps,' she added doubtfully, her eyes lit with mirth. 'I never was much good at drawing,' she admitted, and saw Clive's eyebrows lift a fraction.

'Another imperfection,' he drawled. 'I wonder you'll own to it.'

She laughed and said,

'I'm not perfect by any means, Mr Tarrant.'

'Let me look at the sketch,' he requested, ignoring her comment. 'Yes, it does look attractive. You can take me to it later on.'

This she did, and was elated at his enthusiasm. He asked her if she wanted to pick one of the flowers and press it, and seemed more than a little satisfied when she said no, she felt that it was wrong to pick wild flowers.

'You reduce the number of seeds that will be scattered,' she added. 'And although it's unlikely that anyone else will ever see these, it still seems like vandalism to me to pick them.'

Clive turned his head to look at her. His expression was unreadable, but there was no doubt that he had mellowed considerably during the past twenty-four hours. There was no antagonism about him any more, no sarcasm or contempt in his attitude towards her, although she did wonder just how long this more friendly manner would endure. She naturally allowed her thoughts to fly to the future, cherishing the hope that there might after all be a chance of her working for the Tarrant Line.

She and Clive wandered back along the river bank, chatting and learning something about one another. Faun learned that Clive had already been some distance up the dry river bed, looking for signs of habitation. Some tribes in this primitive *ulu* were still nomadic, clearing ground, cultivating it to produce one single crop, and then moving on again. Clive had hoped to find some evidence of this shifting cultivation, such evidence being proof that Natives did inhabit this region.

'I came upon several streams,' he told Faun as they strolled back to the camp. 'All of them were picturesque in that their banks are different from this. There are flowers in abundance.'

'Flowers?' Faun's eyes brightened. 'What kind?'

'I recognised some of them, but by no means all. I saw calla lilies and arums, many orchids and some small foliage plants.' He looked slantways at her. 'You'd be in your element,' he added, then went on to say that one of the streams was particularly beautiful, as it flowed below a great limestone mass which had been worn away to form a cave.

'Oh ... I must go there! Which way was it?'

'You're not afraid?'

She hesitated a moment, and then, with complete honesty,

'Maybe I am. It was impulsive of me to say I'd go ...'

Faun allowed her voice to trail off, reflecting on Clive's request to be taken to see the wild hibiscus. If only she could make a similar request, and ask to be taken to the cave! She looked up at him from under the thick fringe of her lashes, and saw the sudden quirk of his mouth.

'Well?' he challenged dryly.

Faun blinked at him, feigning surprise and puzzlement.

'Well—what?'

'Come off it, Miss Sheridan! You're not deceiving anyone! You want me to take you to the cave.'

For a space she found speech impossible. This was too good to be true! Were she and Clive Tarrant to be friends after all that had taken place between them? She herself was amazed that she could think of burying the hatchet after all the insults she had received from him. And yet she knew it would be easy to bury it, simply because this man walking beside her was not the arrogant boss of one of the world's most exclusive airlines, but a fellow human being who was sharing the dangers and uncertainties which she herself was experiencing. She said quietly, lifting her beautiful eyes to look at his profile,

'I'd be very grateful if you would take me, Mr Tarrant.'

He did not answer her immediately, and for an uncertain moment she wondered if he would refuse. To her relief he turned his head and smilingly said he would take her the following afternoon.

'It's about a mile and a half, going that way,' he said, pointing in a direction that was at right angles to the river bed along which they were walking.

122

'Is there no fear of getting lost?' she queried, her gaze taking in the tangled mass of vegetation through which they would have to pass.

'I took care to make certain landmarks,' he told her casually. 'For example, there's a great number of sago palms along the way and I took off some of the leaves and turned them upside down to show their lighter undersides. In this way I found no difficulty in picking up my trail.'

'So we're sure of getting back without difficulty?'

'I didn't have any trouble, and I don't anticipate any tomorrow.'

Faun was considering what he had said.

'I believe the pith of sago palms is edible?'

'It is, and we shall be eating it before very long.'

She nodded, then her thoughts leapt back to the journey they would make tomorrow.

'How many miles can one cover in an hour—in this sort of terrain, I mean?'

'Less than a mile when cutting across country like that. Along a stream or game trail it's different.'

'Less than a mile.' She became thoughtful again. 'So we shall have to start out immediately after lunch?'

He nodded.

'If we start out a little after midday we'll have at least five hours of daylight.'

'I'm looking forward to it,' Faun told him with a smile. 'Thank you for agreeing to take me.'

'I'd not have permitted your going alone, Miss Sheridan.'

Permitted ... Why did he have to use such expressions! It was as if he could not resist taunting her, even at this time, when a degree of friendliness had sprung up between them. She saw the shadow of a smile touch his lips and she knew he was waiting for her to retaliate. With admirable restraint she managed to smile and say,

'It would have been risky for me to go alone. I might have met up with one of those Natives you yourself were looking for. She frowned to herself, not at all liking the picture that came before her mental vision— that of Clive coming face to face with a member of some primitive tribe. 'Do you think,' she murmured, speaking her thoughts aloud, 'that it's wise for even two of us to go?'

'Afraid?' He seemed to pounce, almost, as he voiced the word.

Faun shook her head, but not very vigorously, and her face was thoughtful.

'I don't know . . .'

Clive Tarrant's eyebrows lifted with a wry expression.

'You're becoming more feminine every day,' was his satirical comment.

She smiled faintly, recalling her mother's assertion that she was feminine and vulnerable, and wondered what this man would have to say if he were told of it.

'We appear to have gone away from the subject,' she pointed out. 'I was asking if it would be wise to go up to the cave.'

'I've been there already; nothing dramatic happened to me——'

'You could, though, have encountered one of these head-hunters,' she broke in, then added the amendment that although the Natives were supposed to be no longer dedicated to the sport of cutting off heads, they were still uncivilised and therefore were not to be trusted. Clive disagreed, saying that many of the tribes were very civilised, and those who weren't could, for the most part, be relied upon to be friendly.

'As I said earlier,' added Clive thoughtfully, 'we might soon be needing help from one of these tribes.'

Faun shrugged, aware that she had no serious qualms about the visit to the cave ... and the reason was that she had faith in the man standing there, the man she would never have believed she could ever come to like.

She did like him; this was being brought home to her most forcibly as the next few hours went by. The change in his manner, in his regard when he looked at her, the word of appreciation when she produced an appetising evening meal ... all these compounded to form a pleasant feeling for him which erased all that had gone before. Tommy, it was seen, was undoubtedly puzzled by the change; Ingrid was furious over it, glaring at Clive and sending narrowed, wrathful glances in Faun's direction. Malcolm was rather silent during the meal, his eyes often moving from Clive to Faun, with an odd expression in their depths. Faun wondered what he was thinking; perhaps, like her, he was beginning to feel that there might be a chance for Faun, that Clive might after all let her work for him.

When the meal was over Faun and Tommy washed the dishes and stacked them away in the spare hut. Ingrid went to the aircraft while Tommy, working by the light from the fire he had lighted earlier, soon got down to some more work on the chair he was making. It was to be one of five, he had said, although Ingrid had already told him that he need not make one for her.

'I'm far more comfortable in the aircraft,' she said. 'Chairs like that could hardly be comfortable.'

Darkness had fallen and as the sun sank so the air cooled. A large moon appeared above the mountains, and fireflies in the vegetation illuminated it in fitful streaks. There was thunder in the air, but as yet the night was fresh and pleasant and Faun decided to take a stroll along the river bank. But first she dropped in on Malcolm who was reading by the light of a butane lamp. He glanced up with a smile, his eyes running over Faun's attire. Her slacks were now looking the worse for wear, having suffered many 'catches' on thorns and sharp branches and some prickly grass, a large patch of which she had unwittingly entered in her search for edible berries and other fruits. Her shirt was not very clean even though she had washed it that morning. But she dared not use her small tablet of soap for washing clothes, so the rinsing through was more to make her clothes smell sweet than to clean them. The perspiration was one of the discomforts of living in the jungle and she had noticed Tommy and Clive doing a great deal of clothes washing, Tommy doing Malcolm's as well as his own. Ingrid had much more clothing with her than Faun and so she seemed able to keep herself almost immaculate.

.'Not read them all yet?' Faun glanced at the small pile of magazines on the cabinet by Malcolm's bed.

'I've read most of them,' he answered wryly. 'I shall be going through them all again soon.'

'There are some crosswords to do?'

He nodded.

'I ration myself to one a day.'

'I wonder how long we're going to be here.' Faun gave a sigh as she spoke. For herself she was not greatly troubled as yet; for Malcolm, though, she did feel some concern. True, when he was resting like this he seemed fairly comfortable, but when he had been up a while that breathlessness came to him, and the blue tinge to his mouth.

'Clive's thinking of getting help,' she told him.

'From the Natives? He might not find any.'

Malcolm looked at her perceptively.

'Afraid?'

'Not for myself altogether——' This had escaped before she knew it and Malcolm said swiftly, and with an odd inflection in his voice,

'For Clive? Are you afraid for him?'

She found herself colouring slightly.

'I'm anxious, naturally, Malcolm. After all, anyone would be apprehensive of the Natives of Borneo, wouldn't they?'

'I rather think they're more likely to be friendly than otherwise, Faun, and that's why Clive's interested in finding some of them.'

'Mr Tarrant said that if we're not rescued in a day or two he's going up to the confluence; he has an idea he might find a longhouse there.'

Malcolm nodded thoughtfully. He was propped up against the cushions, looking very comfortable, his magazine open on the blanket, a glass of water on the cabinet. The glass, of high quality crystal such as were used in all Clive's aircraft, seemed out of place in this primitive little hut, built as it was of bamboo and palm leaves.

'The Natives always build by water, and especially near a confluence. They travel by boat, you see—*prahus*, they're called, I believe.'

'It will take Mr Tarrant some considerable time to get to the confluence; he'll probably have to cut his way through parts of the jungle.'

Malcolm agreed, a frown creasing his brow.

'This helplessness is getting me down. I could have gone with him had I been fit.'

'Tommy could go, but I have an idea Mr Tarrant will insist that Tommy stays with us. We need someone to stay up all night in case the fires are to be lighted.'

'That's right. As soon as a plane is heard the fires must be lighted, otherwise we'll miss our chance of being spotted.'

Faun stayed with Malcolm a little while longer before, bidding him goodnight, she went from his hut into the sudden blackness of the night. But the moon soon emerged from behind the clouds, bringing some light to the mysterious and primitive landscape of dark jungle vegetation, its luxurious growth flourishing under hothouse conditions, the equatorial climate bathing the whole region in perpetual summer. Faun decided that nowhere on earth could the vegetation be so lavish, so impenetrable, as it was here, in this part of the island of Borneo.

She reached the bank and began strolling along it, her mind occupied with the change that had taken place in Clive Tarrant's attitude towards her. It had meant that life was more pleasant, as the continual animosity which had previously existed between them was little less than a burden in circumstances such as this. The strain was immense for everyone, without the added awareness of being disliked. Faun had carried this awareness and Clive did not understand just how much she was affected mentally by it. Her strength of character was such that she might have coped with the situation as it was, but Faun doubted it. Tension was there, though it might not be apparent, since she had more control over her nerves and emotions than, say, Ingrid.

A sudden sound like the breaking of a twig caused Faun to spin round, every sense alert. A shadow appeared, and a reassuring voice spoke before she had time even to think that it might be a Native approaching her through the tangled mass of undergrowth which closely bordered the bank. Clive had taken a short cut from the camp site to the river's edge.

'You shouldn't be out here alone at night.' His voice was sharp, imperious. 'Supposing you went into the swamp?'

'I didn't think of that. But in any case, it isn't swampy here.'

'You have to mind, though. The swampy patches appear and take you unawares.' Both he and Faun had stopped and were standing reasonably close to one another, two people aware of dangers, vitally conscious of the fact that they could come to a sorry state of health if the rescue were a long time delayed. They both were aware of their surroundings, of the tropical jungle with its teeming life, and its many hazards. Through the darkness came the high-pitched squeak of a bat, one of thousands foraging the air of the jungle. The sound cut through the massed orchestra of cicadas and other noises made by the innumerable inhabitants of this evergreen island whose shores were washed by the lovely South China Sea. It was romantic despite its dangers, a paradise of beauty unexplored, a world lost in its own splendid isolation and remoteness. 'How far were you intending to walk?' Clive's voice drifted into Faun's thoughts and involuntarily she smiled.

'I hadn't given a thought to it. I was going to stroll on until I'd had enough and then turn back.'

'Your absence of fear amazes me,' he said.

'I can experience fear,' she assured him. 'I might as well confess that I felt very afraid when that second engine flamed out.' Her voice was soft and sweetly-toned, her eyes in the moonlight wide and frank and appealing.

'That was understandable.' Clive paused a moment, as if in indecision. But eventually he said, with a sincerity she had never expected to hear from the man she had found so arrogant and insufferable, 'Your control was exceptional, Miss Sheridan. Had I been in charge of the aircraft I couldn't have done any better than you as regards keeping my head.'

So amazed was Faun by this unexpected admission that she found speech impossible for a while. She just stared ahead, into the shadowy recesses made by the folds of the tree-clad hills beyond the bank, her mind confused by Clive's manner with her. Truly he was an enigmatic man. He seemed to be aware of her astonishment and gave her a narrowed smile.

'You surprise me,' she murmured, forestalling the

question which she sensed was hanging on his lips. 'I never expected you to be so honest.'

At this his eyebrows rose a fraction.

'That,' he told her with a hint of the old crispness of tone, 'was not very diplomatic.'

Faun inclined her head in agreement, saying somewhat absently,

'No, I suppose it wasn't.'

Clive relapsed into silence for a while, his eyes gazing into the dark line of the river bed where the plane's wings and fuselage shone in the moonlight. Following the direction of his gaze Faun fell to wondering why Clive had spent so little time with his girl-friend. True, in the daytime he was busy, seeing to Malcolm's needs or helping Tommy. He had explored the immediate territory and wandered further afield; he had assisted with the new shelters, had repeatedly tinkered with the radio and, in fact, had been almost fully occupied. Then of course there was his resting time, which was every other day, as he took it in turns with Tommy to keep an all-night watch for the rescue team. He would come off duty at six or thereabouts and sleep until lunch time. But there were the evenings when he could have gone into the aircraft and kept Ingrid company. Instead, he obviously preferred to stroll like this, in the darkness of the jungle. He spoke at last, his voice drifting into Faun's reflections and bringing her thoughts back to this present moment.

'Would you care to walk on—or were you thinking of turning in?'

A little thrill of pleasure swept through her at the idea of walking with Clive and she answered spontaneously,

131

'I'd love to walk on; it's such a beautiful night.'

'At present, yes, it is, but rain will come, so we'll not stray too far from the camp.' His voice was expressionless and for an instant Faun wondered if he were regretting his invitation, but he was soon assuring her, by his changed tone, that this was not so. 'Watch yourself when we get a little farther along here; there are stinging bushes which can be pretty painful if you happen to step into them.'

Faun had already discovered the truth of this, but she made no mention of it, merely falling into step beside Clive as he sauntered along the narrow grassy verge bordering the bed of the stream. They chatted in a pleasant friendly way, Faun being drawn out as he put questions to her. He realised he had heard of her father, and asked if another pilot of the name of Sheridan was any relation to her family.

'Yes, Father's cousin,' she replied.

'You're a flying family, then?'

'There are several of us,' she answered with a light laugh. 'My uncle on my mother's side was a pilot, but he was killed in a crash.'

'So were my parents,' he told her quietly.

'Oh . . . I'm sorry. Was it a long time ago?'

'I was twelve. My uncle and his wife took me.' He paused and she sensed a bitterness rise within him. 'They were divorced when I was fifteen and I was sent to boarding-school.' He paused again. Faun, his confidence surprising her, made no comment as she felt sure it would not take much to bring his confidences to an abrupt end. He continued after a while, and she learned that his uncle had later died, leaving all he had to Clive. There was no indication in Clive's narrative

132

of the size of the fortune left him, but Faun already knew it was vast. Malcolm had told her this one day when she was in his hut, keeping him company for an hour or so.

'Your childhood was not happy, then?' Faun put in a few words at last, saw Clive nod before saying,

'No, it wasn't, but it's all history now.' He gave her a slantways glance. 'Your childhood appears to have been very happy—from what small items of information you've imparted.'

'It was wonderful,' she returned swiftly. 'We're a most fortunate family——' she broke off and then could not help adding, '—despite the fact of my mother producing two Amazons!'

To her surprise Clive laughed.

'Tell me about your sister,' he said.

Faun obliged, then somehow the conversation drifted back to flying, with Clive making the comment that Faun had been everywhere, that her life up till now must have been rich and varied.

'Yes,' she agreed at once, 'it has. I sometimes sit and reflect on the wonderful sights I've seen.' She turned her head, totally unaware of the beauty of her profile in the moonlight, or that her hair, catching the argent glow, gave her an almost ethereal quality which caught and held her companion's full interest. She had heard an alien sound and was staring into the darkness in front of her, filled with wonderment at the pulsating nocturnal life that was going on all around her. The sound was not repeated and she spoke once more to Clive. 'Have you seen the harbour at Rio?'

'A truly wonderful experience,' he replied.

'And those fantastic bridges at Isfahan?'

'I've seen those too.'

'The Alhambra on a night like this, when the moon is full?'

'Another exceptional experience.'

Faun looked a little doubtfully at him.

'Am I being a bore?' she wanted to know, then was relieved to see him shake his head.

'Certainly not.'

'Travel is a marvellous educator, isn't it?'

'You have an inquisitive mind, Miss Sheridan.'

She reflected on Ingrid's paucity of knowledge about this present environment, on the inane questions she would sometimes ask, and the absurd remarks she would make. How could a man like Clive Tarrant be satisfied with such a girl? Still, Faun thought, he was not really interested in the girl's cultural propensities, but only in her physical attractions.

'I suppose I take after my father,' she remarked at length, looking about her and wondering how far Clive intended to walk. The moon was still bright, but clouds were gathering rather swiftly. 'My mother, too, is always eager to learn.'

'What did she do before her marriage?'

'She was a ballet-dancer.'

'A ballet-dancer!' Clive's glance automatically swept Faun's slender figure. 'You're an interesting family.'

She shrugged slightly.

'I suppose we are a little different from the normal run,' she agreed, but with an edge of modesty to her voice.

'Two pilots, an engineer and a ballet-dancer. Your mother sounds as if she might be the odd one out.'

'If you mean that she's timid, or anything like that,'

said Faun with a laugh, 'then I must disillusion you right away. Mother bosses us all, and that includes my father.'

'You don't resent it, obviously.'

A lovely smile 'it Faun's eyes.

'We wouldn't have her any other way. She's usually right, you see, although we don't always admit that she is. Regarding my appointment with your firm, she said——' Faun stopped abruptly, aware that she had been speaking without thinking.

'Yes?' prompted her companion, coming to a halt and glancing up into the darkening sky.

'Oh—er—nothing.'

The shadow of a smile crossed his face.

'I'm most curious to hear you finish what you were saying, Miss Sheridan.' His voice was soft but insistent, his manner compelling. Faun, unwilling to cause friction between them shook her head vigorously.

'I'd rather not, Mr Tarrant.'

'Perhaps I can guess,' he said musingly after a pause. 'I've an idea your mother would have warned you that you'd not be able to compete with the male applicants.' So smooth the tone, so confident the man was of having made a correct guess. 'Tell me, what had she to say when, after that first interview with my personnel manager, you were told that the job couldn't be given to you because of my attitude towards women pilots?'

'She said she'd warned me; then advised me to forget all about it. It wasn't the only job of its kind, she pointed out.'

'But it was the particular job you wanted, you told me.'

'Yes, it was. I'd heard of the firm, and of the luxury

air limousines you use. I've enjoyed working for a large company but have always wanted to join a smaller, more select airline.' She spoke seriously, stating facts in the way she might state them to someone who was not the boss of the firm about which she was talking. Clive became thoughtful, slanting her a glance now and then, in between casting a look up at the sky. 'I don't understand your attitude, Mr Tarrant,' she could not help adding. 'There's absolutely no reason why a woman can't make as efficient a pilot as a man.'

'I was in a plane piloted by a woman once,' he told her, still in that reflective tone of voice. 'The trouble we ran into was nowhere near as dangerous as that which you encountered, but she panicked. As luck would have it the co-pilot had the sense to take over immediately; otherwise we'd have crashed into the side of a mountain.'

'I expect a man could have panicked in similar circumstances, though.'

'I shouldn't think it very likely.'

'Well, we're arguing about something we'll never be able to answer. I still maintain that women can be as good as men.'

Clive said nothing. Faun turned her head and looked up at him in a thoughtful way, for she sensed a certain bitterness about him and wondered if his mind had switched to his wife. Faun now gained the impression that he had suffered at her hands and also at something his aunt had done to him. He had been bitter when mentioning the divorce that had taken place between her and his uncle. He spoke presently, murmuring almost to himself,

'I suppose my dislike of women goes deeper than——' and then he pulled himself up, his profile set in forbidding lines. Strangely this did not deter Faun from saying, as much to her own surprise as to his,

'You've had a raw deal at some time or another?' Her heartbeats quickened as she waited, noting the mask-like expression that had covered his face. He would resent such a pertinent question, she felt sure, and waited uneasily for his censure. But whatever he had to say was never voiced as Faun suddenly found herself falling, having caught her foot in some roots. Clive sprang forward, hands outstretched, and caught her just as she would have gone headlong into the patch of stinging bushes. She felt his arms about her, strong, protective as they helped her to regain her balance. She felt the hardness of his body against hers, his cool fresh breath on her upturned face. The moment was charged with tension, for instead of releasing her he held her in his arms. Faun knew a simmering of expectancy, a delicious rioting of nerves.

'Faun ...' The name came softly from his lips and then, startling them both, came the first brilliant flash of lightning, followed by an ear-splitting crash of thunder as the violent expansion of air took place. 'We shall have to hurry!' Clive spoke briskly and it seemed that the little scene of unexpected intimacy was nothing more than a figment of Faun's imagination.

CHAPTER EIGHT

IT was only to be expected that Faun felt somewhat shy when on the following morning she met Clive over breakfast. She had awakened to a fleeting sensation of sheer happiness, but immediately on this came the abruptness with which Clive's manner had changed as the lightning warned them both of the urgency of getting back to camp. Her happiness faded, replaced by confusion as she freely owned to herself that what had occurred last evening was not the first occasion on which she had been deeply affected by the magnetic personality of the man she had at first disliked so intensely. What was this new and indefinable jostling of sensations within her mind? Why this feeling of expectancy one moment and of hopelessness the next? More important, why was her career no longer the dazzling star that had shone for so long? Her lovely eyes met Clive's across the table of bamboo at which they both sat ... and she knew that her star had been eclipsed by the man facing her, his eyes all-examining, taking in the dainty colour fluctuating in her cheeks, the tremulous movement of her lips, the bewilderment in her gaze. She knew what he would say even before he opened his mouth.

'What are you thinking about, Miss Sheridan?'

She shook her head, frowning a little.

'You wouldn't be interested, Mr Tarrant.' Faun knew a certain element of dejection that he had called her by her surname. Somehow, she had taken it for granted that having once used her Christian name, he would continue to do so.

'I rather think I would be interested,' he argued, and now his voice carried a hint of sardonic amusement. Faun had the uncomfortable conviction that he was secretly laughing at her shyness, aware as he was of the reason for it. She half wished she had not risen quite so early, as then she and Clive would not be breakfasting alone. But the dawn streaking across the sky had slanted its rays into her hut, and if this was not enough to wake her there had been the cry of gibbons, and the hornbills flapping their ponderous way about, all unconscious that the huts contained humans. Faun had emerged into a world of steaming humidity and was soon recalling the tremendous storm that had occurred the previous night. Rain had lashed at the 'thatch' of palm leaves that roofed her hut; thunder claps had rent the air over and over again, and lightning had repeatedly illuminated the black interior of her shelter. She had lain awake, thinking of Clive, and of Ingrid who of late seemed to alienate herself more and more both from him and the other three who were his companions. 'You haven't answered my question,' said Clive, his quiet voice intruding into her reflections.

'I was thinking about the storm,' she was now able to answer with truth, but his expression of amusement mingling with a tinge of censure told her plainly that he knew she had in fact side-stepped his original query. However, he made no reference to it, merely stating that the storm had been one of the most severe he had ever witnessed. 'Did it keep you awake for long?' he ended, picking up a small piece of biscuit that was his ration and, she noticed, leaving her the piece that was slightly larger. The biscuits were like rusks and there had been an emergency supply of six packets, four of which had already been used.

'I did lie awake for some time,' she answered. 'I wonder how Malcolm went on?'

'I've been in to him; he's sleeping soundly—or was, about a quarter of an hour ago. Tommy was also dead to the world, but then he hadn't been in bed very long.'

'Did he stay up last night? I can't see the necessity when there's that kind of storm raging. We'll not have any rescue team in weather like that.'

'No, but there was no knowing when it would abate. One of us must stay up,' he added gravely. 'You must know that our position's becoming a cause for anxiety?'

'I try not to think about it,' she confessed. 'I never can see the sense in worrying over what I could neither alter nor control.'

'Most sensible,' he agreed, but went on to add, 'I feel we should go out today with the firm intention of looking carefully for signs of habitation. If we do find any tracks or other evidence that Natives might be living hereabouts, then I shall go out early tomorrow and try to reach the confluence.'

'I know that both you and Malcolm are of the opinion that the Natives will be friendly, but it could be otherwise.'

He nodded his head in agreement but his jaw was taut and grim.

'It's a risk I shall have to take, I'm thinking. We haven't any means of communication, with my not being able to get the radio working. We've seen no sign of an aircraft; in view of these things I consider it would be wise for me to do something positive. The Natives usually trade with the peoples of the coast, taking their fruits and other commodities down by *prahu*. I could get help quite easily if I could contact some of these Natives who do this trading.'

'Supposing, though, that they weren't friendly?' Faun little knew just how deep was the frown of anxiety on her brow. Clive looked at it and said, an odd inflection in his voice,

'Am I to take it that you're concerned for my safety?'

She averted her head, aware that she had no wish for him to see the shade of stress that she knew was in her eyes.

'I'd be concerned about anyone who was going into the unknown like that. Apart from anything else, there are other dangers.'

He nodded.

'Snakes and the honey bear, eh?'

'If Tommy could go with you——' she began, but Clive interrupted her.

'Tommy is needed at the camp,' he told her abruptly.

Faun never did know what made her say,

'I could come with you, Mr Tarrant.'

A deep and profound silence fell between them, with Clive surprising her by his total lack of emotion of any kind. In fact, amazing as it seemed, he appeared to be considering her suggestion in some depth. She waited, conscious of a certain degree of excitement; she knew she would feel strangely honoured if such a man could put that sort of reliance on her. He looked at her, his eyes flickering over her face and figure as if assessing her worth in an emergency. That she would keep cool was plain, or it should be by now. To her great satisfaction he nodded thoughtfully and said yes, he would accept her offer. Later, as Faun was clearing away the breakfast dishes, he came up to her and said,

'I feel we ought to go on the trek today, Miss Sheridan. What I mean is, we oughtn't to return and then set out again tomorrow for the confluence. It can be done today if we set out now.'

'Immediately?' She was quite agreeable, she went on to add, but there must be some preparation. 'We'll need to take some food and water.'

'Of course.' He hesitated a moment. 'And other things, Miss Sheridan.'

'Other things?'

'If it should happen that the way through the jungle is more difficult than I anticipate, we might not be able to get back tonight.'

'I see.' She was coolly weighing these words of his, while he stood there, tall and aristocratic, in clothes much the worse for wear, waiting for her to speak. 'We could take two parachute canopies for shelters, couldn't we?'

Clive seemed to smile, for his lips took on a slightly crooked look.

'Nothing seems to daunt you,' he said. And before she could comment, 'Yes, the parachute canopies would come in useful in that kind of an emergency.'

Faun set to at once to prepare food for the journey. She also filled two flasks with tea and one with soup which she emptied from a tin and heated on the butane stove. Clive made a rucksack of sorts from the moquette cover he took off a cushion. Then, with everything prepared, he went over to Malcolm's shelter and spent about five minutes with him. When he emerged he said abruptly,

'Malcolm's been given all the instructions. He'll tell Ingrid, when she wakes, what we've decided to do. Tommy won't be up yet, of course, but Malcolm will get up at once and be alert to wake Tommy if he should hear an aircraft flying over.'

Faun's eyes went to the several piles of dry wood and leaves that the men had made ready to light. A can of aircraft fuel stood ready by each unlighted fire.

'Did Malcolm approve of what we intended doing?' Faun asked the question while watching Clive fixing the rucksack to his back. She herself carried a holdall containing such things as toothbrush and other toilet requisites. The holdall had a conveniently long handle, so she could sling it over her shoulder.

'No, he doesn't,' answered Clive, but with a casual air that told her at once that any protests which Malcolm had thought fit to make had been rejected without even a trace of interest. Clive took up the axe he had ready, looked around for a moment before allowing his eyes to linger on the shining wings and fuselage of the plane, and then asked Faun if she was ready.

She nodded, falling into step beside him as he began to stride out, making for the dry river bed. They crossed it then took the path at right angles to it which Clive had previously pointed out. However, it was not a path in the true sense of the word, but merely a direction, with some slight evidence of Clive's progress

143

through it, the undergrowth being still laid low here and there where he had trampled it down.

'We've made a very early start,' he was saying after a while. 'I'm glad we made the decision.'

'Yes, so am I.' She didn't add to this, but had she been able to say what was in her mind then Clive would have learned that the idea of a whole day in his company was just as exciting to her as the idea of finding a Native settlement where help could be obtained. She naturally found herself thinking of Ingrid, and wondering whether the girl would be angry at the idea of Faun's going off like this with her boy-friend. Faun decided that the way Ingrid was at present she would not care one way or the other what Clive Tarrant did.

'We'll soon have to begin leaving our trail.' Clive's voice cut into the silence that had dropped and Faun looked around.

'Shall I break off some of these leaves?' she asked, noticing some rather large leaves which were much lighter on their undersides than on top. He said yes, but he himself raised the axe and blazed a tree as he passed it.

The time passed pleasantly, but both travellers were becoming hot and very dusty. The sun was climbing; though as the jungle thickened, away from the narrow strip which bordered the river, the sun's rays did not penetrate. Humidity, though, was high, with steam beginning to rise with the gradual increase in the sun's heat. They stopped on reaching the cave of which Clive had spoken and Faun gasped at the beauty of the workings of nature in carving out the cave and decorating it with fantastic shapes.

'It's a pity we can't stay and explore,' she said, but

added, 'We ought not to waste much time here at all, not in view of our changed plans.'

Clive was advancing before her and suddenly she heard an exclamation issue from his lips.

'A sherd of earthenware!' Clive bent to look for more. Faun, fascinated, automatically took the sherd from his hand.

'It's Chinese ...' She looked up on hearing another exclamation. 'What is it?'

'A sort of wooden paddle.' He turned to her and she saw the excitement in his eyes. 'Evidence of habitation,' he said, 'but habitation of prehistoric times!'

'Prehistoric?' Faun glanced at the piece of pottery in her hand. 'I should have thought that this was to be dated about 900 A.D.,' she said.

'That, yes, perhaps. But this ...' He went forward; she asked how these things had escaped him on his earlier visit. 'I wasn't in this particular grotto.' He glanced around. 'This limestone massif must be riddled with caves. Just look——' He spread a hand and in the dim half-light Faun could see one dark opening after another. 'It reminds one of a piece of Gruyère cheese,' said Clive. 'Are you game for a little exploring?'

'Of course.' She was so excited that she forgot for the moment the real object of their trek through the deep dark jungle. For here was evidence of cavemen's life and there was no knowing what might be discovered. 'We'll have to leave a trail, through.'

As a matter of fact Clive was already taking a large ball of string from his pocket.

'What served in the labyrinth of Crete can serve here.'

'Where did you find that string?' Faun wanted to

know, 'I could have done with it when Tommy was making my bed.'

'It was in the aircraft. I knew I'd find a better use for it than what Tommy could do with it. Besides, it made him improvise.'

'How far shall we go?' Faun was asking about five minutes later when she was closely following Clive into the dim dark cave, his torch shining on the walls. Lime-water dripped incessantly from the ceiling in one particular part, a crack obviously occurring somewhere in the rocks above.

'Not too far. I wonder, Faun, if we're the first people to visit this cave since it was abandoned by whoever originally occupied it.'

Faun . . . So naturally this had come out. She thought of his love of natural things that they both shared; it had surely been this that had dissolved the animosity which had in the beginning been so strong within them both.

'It's an awesome thought. We might find a burial place.'

'In this climate bones don't last too long unless protected by, say, the limestone which is dripping down, carried in the water.' He was carrying on, having bent to take up some object which he slipped into his pocket. 'It's a pity we haven't the time to make a more thorough exploration,' he said. 'Would you enjoy that?'

'Very much,' was Faun's enthusiastic reply, and suddenly her companion laughed.

'What a remarkable young woman you are! Ninety-nine out of a hundred would be scared out of their wits.'

Was he thinking of Ingrid? she wondered.

146

'I find anything like this far too exciting for me to be scared. Besides, there's nothing alive here, so we couldn't come to any harm.' Nevertheless, she found herself looking down, making sure that the string was still there. Clive shone his torch all around, and to Faun's amazement a painting came to light. Clive saw it at the same time as she, and kept his torch directed upon it. 'Oh ...!' she gasped. 'What have we found, Clive?' She did not even know she had addressed him thus, nor did he let her see, even by a gesture, that he resented it. In fact, it was of scant importance in a situation such as this, where two people had come upon a cave painting that had been executed thousands of years ago by the peoples who had inhabited Borneo long before the Dyaks and Ibans and other tribes whose territory it now was.

Clive was moving closer to the wall of the cave, his torch lighting up the painting, which stood out clearly against the glistening white limestone of the rock on which it had survived for aeons of time, unseen by man, a treasure there for Faun and Clive to discover. She was awed, breathless as she stood and looked. She asked at last how it had been done.

'In red haemite,' he answered, 'which as you know is iron ore.'

'Weren't they clever?' She was close to Clive—in fact, her hand was touching his as she lifted it to point. He seemed not to notice the contact, but Faun did. It was like an electric vibration shooting through her whole body. What was this new and wonderful feeling within her? She had the predominant sensation of being swept irresistibly along a path which, though not of her own choosing, was nevertheless offering the most pleasant travel she had ever experienced.

'Very clever. I'm sure there was a high flowering of ritual life here in Borneo in those far off times.'

'It makes you wonder whether there was once a civilisation even superior to ours today.'

'I wouldn't go that far, but I do feel that we know scarcely anything about the civilisation that existed here at one time.' As he spoke he again picked out something on the floor and, stooping to take it in his hand, he slipped it into his pocket and Faun heard it rattle against the first object he had put there.

'Forgotten times ... and people ...' Faun spoke mechanically, her wide intelligent brow furrowed. 'What were they like? Was this land as it is today—dense jungle? Or was it a much more friendly place, with pastures and low hills?' She continued to murmur, to herself, while her companion, unmoving now, listened, the most inscrutable expression on his face. The silence, the intimacy of being in this forgotten dwelling place of people long dead and whose bones, even, had come to dust, the knowledge that no one in the whole world knew they were here ... all this made for a situation where Clive and Faun were bound to become close. And when at length Clive swung around with the intention of returning to the mouth of the main cave, there was a strange smile upon his lips, and his hand touched Faun's as he said,

'You're a strange girl, Faun, but a darned interesting one!'

Something inside her warmed deliciously; she responded to his smile, even though she doubted very

148

much that he could be aware of this, since he was now busily winding up the string, having handed the torch to Faun.

The dry entrance to the main cave at last being reached, they stepped out into the steaming jungle again. A gibbon's *wak-wak-wak* cut the silence; a Proboscis monkey looked down from the low branch of a tree, a shy creature, protected from captivity because of its delicate constitution which invariably caused it to die if taken from its natural habitat.

'What an experience that was!' Faun turned to Clive with a happy smile on her face. 'I'd love to come back one day and explore. Do you suppose one could organise an expedition?'

'I should think the government of Sarawak would have something to say about that, Faun. I have a feeling that many of the caves are at the present time being explored by the proper authorities.'

'I know the Niah caves have been explored. They've found marvellous things in those.' She stopped for a moment. 'What did you pick up?' she wanted to know, her glance moving automatically to his pocket.

Clive produced the two objects: a piece of carved bone and a polished cutting tool.

'There must be numerous such finds,' he said, handing the objects to Faun after having spent a few minutes examining them.

'Would these be Neolithic?'

'Perhaps; it's difficult to say.'

After a while they went on, Clive sometimes having to hack a way through the tangled mass of jungle vegetation. Another cave appeared and with a glance at one another both Faun and Clive decided they could not resist taking a look. They had not proceeded far when Clive said,

'Look up there!' and shone his torch on to the ceiling.

'Oh ...!' Faun looked up at what must have been millions of bats. 'I've heard of them, but never, never expected to see a sight like this!'

'Incredible, isn't it?' Even Clive seemed overawed at the sight. His eyes moved eventually to the floor. On it was an endless supply of guano which, he told Faun, could in some caves accumulate to a depth of a hundred feet or more.

'The swiftlets contribute to this guano, of course.' Clive nodded.

'The swifts come in at dusk when the bats go out.'

Faun found the smell becoming too much for her and said apologetically that she would rather not explore this particular cave. Clive laughed, slanting her a wry glance.

'I agree with you,' he said, 'this is more than a little overpowering.'

The whole area was honeycombed with caves; this they discovered as they progressed north-eastwards, making for the confluence of which Clive had spoken.

'Everywhere you look you see caves!' Faun could not help exclaiming, even though Clive had already mentioned this. 'Just look up at this limestone outcrop. There must be hundreds of grottoes and corridors inside it.'

'And plenty of evidence of the intense activities of stone-age peoples,' supplemented Clive thoughtfully.

'They not only lived in such caves but used them for burials and rituals.'

'Clive ... isn't there a lot we don't know about this world of ours?'

He turned to her, smiling, and she thought that she had never seen a more attractive man in her life—this despite his mud-bespattered clothes with their various tears and 'pulls'. His face was sun-bitten, his hair looked tough, and in need of soap, as did her own, for that matter.

'There is indeed, Faun, yet people like you and me are among the most fortunate in that we do get around more than most. As you were saying the other day, you've seen some wonderful sights.'

She nodded and observed reflectively,

'Yes that's very true. But never have I seen anything like this——' She broke off and a light laugh escaped her. 'It's almost worth being stranded in the jungle for!'

He agreed.

'If it weren't for Malcolm I'd not mind very much if our rescue was delayed. But although it might seem that Malcolm is improving, I'm very much afraid that this is not the case.'

'I myself have had my doubts,' she admitted. 'At times his breathing's most difficult isn't it?'

'Yes and that bluish tinge comes very readily to his lips with only the slightest amount of exertion on his part.'

They walked on for another half hour and then Clive said it was time for their midday snack. Finding a flat ledge near the entrance to another cave, he discarded

151

the rucksack, whereupon Faun opened it and took out some of the contents. All around was the teeming, humid jungle, with only the cave entrance dry and clear of vegetation. To Faun's delight a baby orang-utan came out of a thicket, and a moment later its mother appeared. Faun and Clive had settled down with their snack, and a silence had fallen between them. So the most famous of all Borneo animals had come out, unaware that his closest of all cousins—*Homo sapiens*—was being delighted by the antics of mother and baby.

'Oh, weren't they sweet!' Faun spoke when at last it was plain that the animals, having disappeared, were not coming back. 'I adore them!'

Clive turned his head, eyeing her in a thoughtful way. She could not help contrasting this man with that arrogant, egotistical person who had so contemptuosly refused to admit that women could fly planes with the same safety and efficiency as men.

'I once remarked that you were becoming more feminine every day.' Clive's quirk of humour which accompanied these words only added to the attractiveness of his appearance. 'I find that you're in fact very feminine at times.'

'What about the Amazon?' she could not resist asking, a hint of mischief in her voice which she would never have used before—at least, not when speaking to Clive.

'Ah, the Amazon?' He pretended to become engrossed in reflection. 'She seems to be more concerned with flying than with anything else.'

Faun laughed.

'In other words, I'm feminine when not engaged in

anything to do with my job?' Clive merely nodded and Faun found herself saying, 'Mother always maintained I had a dual personality.' And then she stopped, for whenever she thought of her parents, and especially her mother, she felt a pang of anxiety, for although she was in fact enjoying herself at this time, she knew that her mother would be almost out of her mind with worry.

'She did? Tell me about your mother,' he invited.

'She's the loveliest person imaginable.'

'And doesn't mind that her daughters do men's jobs?'

'She has never interfered with our ambitions. Nevertheless, she does regret our not having anything to do with men—by that, I mean, she would like us to marry and provide her with grandchildren. Her friends have these grandchildren visiting them at the week-ends and Mother feels rather left out of it.'

Clive's lips twitched.

'You don't have anything to do with men, you say?'

She coloured, unaware that she was appearing most attractive to this man sitting beside her, in this 'lost-world' jungle, this primary rain forest where nature reigned supreme.

'I've never had time for dates and dances,' she said.

'Dates and dances ...' His expression altered, becoming serious and a little stern. 'You should never allow your work to dominate your whole life, Faun. There are other things to do, other pleasures to partake of.'

'Meaning?' She spoke the one word softly, thinking of Ingrid and the affair that had clearly gone on between her and Clive, a purely physical relationship, Faun had decided right at the start.

'Meaning dates and dances, as you so aptly put it. The company of the opposite sex can be very pleasurable.'

She smiled faintly.

'I suppose I'm not one for dallying,' she commented seriously. 'I told Mother that when the right one comes along I shall give him my most careful consideration.'

'Good lord! What did your mother have to say to a statement like that?'

'She said,' answered Faun with a laugh, 'that I'd frighten him away if I took that sort of a businessiike attitude.'

'She's right, too! Careful consideration indeed! You have a lot to learn about love my girl!'

Love ... She slanted a glance at his profile, memory bringing back the various occasions when this man had affected her senses. and just a short while back, when their hands had touched ... She felt the colour mount her cheeks, knew again that warmth she knew when Clive had said she was a strange girl but an interesting one. She recalled that her career had no longer been the one shining star on her horizon, that it had been eclipsed by a man who, she had once thought had erected an invincible barrier between them, this owing to his intense dislike of women.

She found herself asking about his aunt, aware that she was 'fishing', desirous of hearing something about his wife as well. He. like Faun herself, appeared to be affected by the isolation and primitive surroundings in that he became expansive, just as she herself had been.

154

She sat quietly and listened, learning that his aunt had gone off with another man. His uncle had been so shattered that he had put Clive into a boarding-school and gone off to travel the world. Clive had, therefore, suffered a second upheaval in his childhood. He paused after this and as Faun looked at the hard and bitter outline of his profile she felt a great wave of sympathy sweep over her. She recalled her own happy childhood. She and her sister had never known anything but love, deep, deep love, and this had come from both her parents, who had an extremely strong sense of parental obligation.

After a while Clive glanced at his watch and Faun accepted that his confidences had come to an end. But she was mistaken, as he began to speak again, saying very quietly,

'I married when I was twenty-three. It was doomed from the start.'

Faun tried to speak, but words were difficult. At length, though, she managed to say, wisely keeping any trace of pity out of her voice,

'Twenty-three is far too young for a man to marry.'

'Of course it is,' matter-of-factly. 'But I suppose I was desperate for some kind of stability. A wife and a home usually provide a man with that kind of stability.'

'Yes ...' Faun looked at him, her brow furrowed a little. Strangely, his admissions had not seemed astonishing to her, for they fitted in with this intimate situation of two people alone in an environment such as this. 'Your wife ... she is still living?'

'I have no idea,' came his indifferent reply. 'We were divorced eight years ago, three years after the marriage.'

155

Bitterness drew lines across his face again; Faun wanted desperately to say something that would erase them.

'It's in the past, Clive, and shouldn't be troubling you any more.'

'It isn't.' And yet the bitterness remained. 'I expect it was my fault as much as hers. After all, it takes two to make a quarrel.'

'You quarrelled a great deal?'

For a space he seemed miles away from her.

'About three times a week.'

'Good lord!' exclaimed Faun before she could stop herself. 'Three times a week? What a life! My sister and I have never known our parents to have one really serious quarrel. Some disagreements occur from time to time, of course, but they kiss and make up long before it becomes serious.' Faun's lovely eyes were meditative; Clive, watching her, shook his head, as if he had just witnessed something which he could not fully comprehend. 'Three times a week!' she cried again. 'Oh, but life must have been hell.'

'It was, Faun.' Clive paused a moment. 'I suppose I don't owe my wife any loyalty, so I'll tell you that she was virtually a nymphomaniac in that her desire for men was insatiable.' So quietly he spoke, and without any emotion now. It was as if Faun had affected him by her silent sympathy, and by her understanding, revealed—perhaps unconsciously—by her horrified exclamations.

'And you've never thought of a second marriage?'

'Not until——" Clive stopped himself with an abruptness which startled Faun. 'No,' he said presently, 'I haven't thought of a second marriage.' But something in his tone caught her attention. What was it? She felt she ought to be able to grasp it, to derive some information from it. He had been speaking in the past tense ... Faun's brow creased; she still felt she was missing something vital that had underlain his quite ordinary statement. The past tense? Well, what could be derived from that? Nothing that Faun could see. She was still frowning when Clive's brisk voice broke into her thoughts. 'We must move, Faun, if we're to get to that confluence and back before nightfall.'

'Shall we be able to do it?'

'I think so; the going's not so difficult as I'd imagined. This axe seems to cope with anything that gets in our way.'

'And it's been most useful in blazing the trees.'

'If you'll pack up the rucksack I'll take another look at the map. I might of course be mistaken, but I feel fairly confident that we're somewhere close to that confluence.' They were actually on one of the banks of an affluent, having come upon it unexpectedly after meeting a deep gorge and numerous rapids.

He seemed satisfied after taking a close and prolonged look at the map. Faun had packed up and was waiting patiently for him to fold up the map. This he did, tucking it into the rucksack before hitching it up on to his back.

'Ready?' he smiled, and Faun nodded. She fell in by his side and together they strode on, through the dense forest where heavy rainfall and hot sunshine conspired to produce the extravagant growth of vegetation through which they were having to travel.

CHAPTER NINE

THE longhouse came into view through the trees, although as yet it was a good distance away.

'Your hunch was right!' Faun, excited and yet apprehensive, was the first to spot the Native village—the long communal building that housed the entire tribe. 'What shall we do now, Clive?'

He had stopped, as if undecided.

'I shouldn't have brought you,' he said almost harshly. 'I don't know what possessed me to be persuaded.'

Gasping at this unexpected unfriendliness, Faun could only stare, conscious of a sinking feeling in the region of her heart.

'I—I didn't try to—to persuade you,' she quivered, almost like a child bewildered by sudden ill-treatment. 'I merely made the—the suggestion.'

He looked at her through hard eyes.

'You're going to be an encumbrance!'

'No such thing! I don't know how you can say so.'

'We don't know what these people will be like.'

'You said they'd be friendly, and so did Malcolm.'

'I said they're more likely to be friendly than hostile,' he argued irritably. 'I ought to have had more sense than to bring you.'

'I'm sorry,' she said stiffly, but her mouth still quivered with the hurt she was experiencing. 'If you like I can turn around and make my way back.'

'Don't be such a damned fool! Do you suppose I'd allow you to go all that way on your own?'

Her beautiful eyes challenged in spite of the fact that tears were very close.

'You couldn't stop me,' she countered.

'No?' glintingly. 'Just you try and get away, my girl, and you'll be sorry!'

'Threats again? I'd taken it for granted that you'd mellowed, but it seems I've made a mistake!'

Clive glowered at her. His friendliness seemed never to have happened, for this was the man she had first known.

'Let's not fight at this time,' he said, rather more quietly. 'A plan of action will be more profitable.'

'You said you'd get help.'

'If I'd been on my own I'd have gone up to the longhouse, yes, but now——' He broke off, glowering at her again. She was stung to saying,

'Don't let me stop you! I can stay here.'

'You think I would leave you?'

'Well—er—no.'

Exasperatedly he said,

'Then why the devil come out with such nonsensical suggestions!'

'Are we going up to that place?' she inquired coldly. 'We can't stand here much longer. You do realise, I suppose, that we've taken far longer in getting here than we expected?'

'Don't be absurd! Of course I know!'

Deflated, Faun lapsed into silence. But suddenly the tears came and she sought swiftly for a handkerchief. She was vitally aware of pain, of a feeling of bitter disappointment ... for she had by now admitted that she was head over heels in love with Clive and that every sharp word cut her like the point of a sword.

'I th-think you should go on alone——'

'Crying?' He seemed dazed by what he saw. 'Well, well, yet another sign of femininity.'

'This is no time for sarcasm!'

'Here, take this. It's not over-clean, but you might find a patch that will do.' He held out his handkerchief. She accepted it, dried her eyes and cheeks, blew her nose vigorously and held it out to him again. He took it gingerly, and laughed. 'You were saying,' he murmured with a strange inflection, 'that your parents always kissed and made up before a disagreement became a quarrel.' He gave her no time to do anything except look bewilderedly at him before he drew her close—not too gently at all—and kissed her hard on the mouth. 'A most excellent idea, especially when you've no time to quarrel anyway. Sit down and we'll think what we must do.'

She obeyed, dazed herself by his unexpected action. His face was set, his eyes staring ahead to the building which could just be discerned in the distance. A long-house. And within its palm-thatched walls were Natives ... who had, not so very long ago, made good sport of collecting heads. They made their kill with the poison dart from a blowpipe, then with that evil-looking knife called a *parang*, they sliced off the victim's head which they carried triumphantly back to their abode where it was hung up, a gory trophy, among a dozen or so other trophies of a similar design.

She looked at Clive, who had laid down one of the

parachute canopies for them to sit on. Behind him were shadows cast by trees and other vegetation, and he appeared gaunt to her, and formidable, too tall by far, too masculine, too stern. He sat down presently beside her, his expression thoughtful, and undecided. She waited, her mind going back to the past couple of hours and the terrain through which they had fought their way. Dense undergrowth alternating with shady recesses in which the forest hoarded its rarer treasures—floral treasures like the exquisite orchids that flourished in abundance. Beautiful and languid, they often dangled in mid-air, suspended from the branches to which they were attached. Clive had told her there were hundreds of species growing in Sarawak and other parts of the island of Borneo. Some, she had noticed, were fancifully shaped, and tinted with strange and magnificent colours. She and Clive had also come across the fantastic pitcher plants, those rare beauties with the reputation for devouring insects. Sometimes a clearing had come unexpectedly and Clive would state quite firmly that here was evidence of some wandering tribe—perhaps the Punans who never made any permanent camp, but just wandered about the jungle, eating grubs and fruits and sometimes a wild pig they had managed to catch. When these clearings appeared the sky appeared also, a blue and white canopy ornamented with floating clouds. Clive had found some stick insects, those creatures made by nature in the image of twigs. Faun had called his attention to some gorgeous butterflies, while later on he had brought to *her* attention a couple of small spider-hunters, charming little birds with green bodies and long curving beaks.

Altogether it had been a most pleasant and interesting trek, and now, she thought as she looked at Clive, it had ended by his being angry with her . . . and then kissing her. What an unpredictable man he was! The kiss of course meant nothing more than what he had said it was to mean—the friendly gesture that was to prevent a quarrel. But Faun could still feel it, as if the hard pressure was still there, even now.

At last Clive spoke, breaking into her musings.

'We'll go back, Faun, and tomorrow I shall come up here alone.'

'Alone?' Something within her stirred, like a hint of fear. 'No—please let's go there now—together.' Entreaty mingled with concern; he was bound to notice and a strange frown settled between his eyes.

'I'm not taking you over there,' was his firm rejoinder. 'It's an unpredictable situation and I'm not intending to lead you into a danger which can obviously be avoided. Come,' he added briskly, glancing at his watch, 'let's start. Even if we hurry we can't possibly be back before dark, but at least we shall be able to put some considerable distance between us and this village.'

Faun bit her lip, aware that had she not been with Clive he would have gone up to the longhouse and tried to converse with the Natives there.

She rose from her sitting position and watched him as he folded the canopy and put it into his rucksack. She said, as they began to retrace their steps,

'When we first started out you had every intention of contacting any Natives we might meet.'

'That's true. But as there's the risk of their not being friendly I've decided not to risk your safety.'

'What about yours?' she cried. 'Tomorrow, going there all alone!'

He turned to look curiously at her.

'I shall be all right,' he assured her.

'Then so shall I,' she pointed out reasonably. 'If they're friendly then we shall both be all right.'

'And if they're not then I alone will be in danger.'

'But you've just said you'll be all right!' She was angry because of her fear, and she actually wanted to dictate to him, to tell him he could not go alone! It was absurd and yet she felt she had the *right* to voice her strong protest. 'I don't want you to go alone, Clive.' The plea was in her voice again. Clive stopped and took hold of one of her hands. It was clammy, and it was unsteady. His voice was gentle all at once, as he said, his deep-set blue eyes intently fixed upon her face, taking in its pallor, and the tremulous quivering of her lips,

'Can't you see, Faun, that I can't let you go up there?'

'But this morning—you weren't in this frame of mind then.' She was conscious of his touch, of his nearness, of the strange gentleness that characterised his whole demeanour.

'I must confess, Faun, that I didn't give sufficient thought to the matter. I suppose I was fully convinced that the Natives—should we happen to meet any— would be friendly towards us.'

'And now you have doubts?'

He made no immediate answer, but absently stroked the back of her hand with his thumb.

'I can't honestly say I have doubts, but I'm not as sure as I was then.'

She frowned at him.

163

'I wish you'd be a little more explicit,' she complained fractiously. 'I don't understand you at all.'

A faint smile lifted the corners of his mouth.

'No, Faun, I don't suppose you do,' was all he said, and then, letting go of her hand, he began to walk on again.

Several hours had gone by since the longhouse had been sighted, and by now Faun and Clive should have been nearing the camp. But a terrible storm had raged, driving them into one of the caves, where they had been forced to remain until long after darkness had set in. Clive decided they must stay where they were, for it was impossible to find his marked trees even with the aid of his powerful torch.

'Sleep in a cave?' shuddered Faun. 'I shall be terrified!'

'Terrified?' In spite of the discomfort of their position Clive had to laugh. 'My dear girl, you're talking the greatest nonsense! You, who managed to keep as cool as you like in that emergency, are trying to tell me you're afraid of sleeping in a cave?'

'It's different,' she complained, shuddering again as she thought of all those bats. Reading these thoughts, Clive was quick to remind her that the bats would have all gone and nothing more frightening than the swiftlets would be occupying the cave.

'Come on, let's have a meal of sorts before we turn in.'

'I'd rather stay outside, if you don't mind.'

'I do mind. For one thing it's far too wet. You might be walking on the bottom of a lake the way this ground

164

is after that downpour. No, the cave offers us shelter from another possible storm, and protection from night prowlers of one kind or another.'

'Snakes and things might come in,' she said.

'They don't often come into the caves, Faun. In any case, I'm here and you've only to shout out if anything startles you in the night.' So cool and composed! Faun felt safe all at once and made no further demur about sleeping in the cave.

'But you won't go far away?' she begged.

'No, of course I won't.' Clive paused and looked at her in the darkness. 'You're not nearly so tough as you appeared at first, my dear.'

My dear ... It sounded nice even though it meant nothing much at all.

'Mother says the same thing.'

'The same thing?'

'That I'm not so tough as people believe.' She stopped rather abruptly and even though she could not see his features she knew instinctively that his expression was one of sudden amusement.

'You mean, I think, that your mother says you're not so tough as you'd have people believe?'

'Yes, that's what I said.'

'No, you didn't!' Clive actually gave her a playful slap. 'The food, my child, and then for some rest. We shall be on our way at six in the morning, immediately the dawn breaks, that is.'

Faun got out the food, and the flask containing the last of the tea she had made. Clive spread the parachute canopies over the floor of the cave, finding a place close to the entrance that was comparatively free of anything

165

but the actual limestone deposits. It would be a hard uncomfortable bed, he warned, but at least they would be dry.

'If you're cold in the night let me know and you can have my canopy over you,' he said.

'And let you sleep on the stone floor?' Faun shook her head emphatically. 'I shall manage very well, Clive, thank you all the same.'

'We'll see.' He propped the torch so that it would give ample light for them to eat by. Faun, though not now in the least happy, still felt a certain degree of pleasure at being with Clive. It was a comradely situation, and she felt very safe, sure that he would not fail her if she did happen to ask for his help during the night.

But it was not help she wanted, but warmth. The early hours were perishing; she shivered for a long while before saying, very softly in case she should wake him if he were asleep,

'Clive ...'

'Yes.' The answer came promptly, assuring her that he was already awake.

'Are you cold?'

'Very.'

'Perhaps I should get up and jump about—or something.'

'No, I have a better idea altogether.'

'I'm not taking your canopy,' she returned firmly.

'I haven't offered it.' He was closer now, and she felt his breath on her cheek. 'There are times, Faun, when all inhibitions must be cast away. We need to lie close in order to conserve the warmth from both our bodies. You understand?'

She shook her head at first, but as a great shiver rippled though her body she said yes, she understood.

'Come on, then.' Clive moved right up to her and lay on her canopy, doubling his own and putting it over them both. His arms came about her shivering body; she felt the warmth of his coming through to her, and she relaxed when ordered to. 'Are you more comfortable now?' His voice, soft and distinctly hoarse, frightened her a little; she was well aware of the risk involved in a position of intimacy such as this. But the sheer ecstasy of it flooded her being and everything else dissolved beside it.

'Yes,' she whispered, making no attempt to move her face from where it was, against his. 'I'm very comfortable indeed.'

'You'll be warm in a few minutes.' Clive's lips were almost touching hers, so that his clean fresh breath mingled with her own. She lay still, tensed until ordered once again to relax. Clive's arms tightened; she was brought closer still ... and closer ...

The night was over and dawn penetrated the mass of tangled jungle vegetation. Clive wakened and stretched luxuriously, his eyes on the lovely serene face beside him. He whispered her name and a smile fluttered to her lips. And then she was wide awake and sitting upright, blushing painfully as memory flooded over her.

'I—I——'

'No time for chatting, I'm afraid,' broke in Clive briskly. 'We must be on our way.' And so the embarrassment was gone as quickly as it had come and Faun threw him a grateful glance. He smiled and she responded, her cup full of happiness. She rose and washed

167

in the stream, then unpacked the rucksack while Clive, also having washed in the stream, folded the parachute canopies and put them away. Breakfast was merely a couple of biscuits each, a small piece of chocolate and clear cold water from the stream. 'You're getting thin,' Clive observed when they had finished and were ready to move on. 'Let's hope we shall soon have help.'

She said,

'I don't want you to go alone, Clive. Please take Tommy. I'll stay awake at night and be ready to light the fires.'

'I'll bet you would, too!' he exclaimed, and there was no doubting the admiration in his voice.

'Will you let Tommy accompany you?' she persisted.

'No, child, I will not. Should anything happen——' He broke off sharply, frowning in vexation at his own slip. Faun seized on it, as he feared she would.

'So you are in doubt! Clive, I beg of you, don't go alone!'

'To be quite blunt about it, Faun, if those Natives are not friendly, then there's no darned sense in two of us running into danger.'

She bit her lip till it hurt. Terror looked out of her eyes when she raised them to his.

'Neither of you need go. Tommy will probably have caught that pig he was after, so we'll not be short of food. We'll be found sooner or later——'

'You're forgetting about Malcolm,' broke in Clive quietly. 'His condition will deteriorate very quickly if he doesn't get medical attention soon.'

She nodded her head. It was true; she had forgotten about Malcolm in her anxiety for Clive.

'You're determined to go,' she said, more to herself than to him.

'Yes, Faun, I am——' He broke off and spun around. 'What was that?'

'I didn't hear anything ...' Faun's voice failed her and for the very first time in her life she was numbed with fear. Coming towards them from the rear were five Natives, all carrying *parangs* in their hands. They moved silently, their long, lank black hair framing faces with Mongoloid characteristics—wide cheekbones and small oblique eyes with that peculiar fold of the upper eyelid at the nasal end. Their noses were wide at the nostrils, their lips broad and thick. Their only clothing was a loincloth, but in their ears they wore leopard fangs or hornbill earrings and round their necks they wore brightly-coloured beads and other ornaments, some made of brass. They were dark-skinned but by no means black; their bodies shone as if smeared with oil. Faun felt the blood pounding in her ears as the men drew near.

'Well,' said Clive at his calmest, 'it seems that fate has taken a hand and that we're to meet the Natives of the village after all.'

Faun was still dumb, and frozen into immobility. She and Clive just stood there, waiting for the five Natives to come up to them. One spoke, uttering guttural sounds. Clive listened intently when another spoke. Faun saw his eyes become alert.

'You understand the language?' she managed at last through lips that were stiff and dry.

'Malay. I had an idea that they'd be using that language. And it wouldn't surprise me if one or two don't understand English. It all depends if these people are traders with those of the coast.' He waited another second or two and then, stepping forward fearlessly he addressed the Natives in Malay. Their expressions did not change and yet Faun knew that they understood. Clive spoke again, pointing to the sky, and then to her and himself. One of the Natives nodded and then—bringing such a flood of relief to Faun that she felt she would collapse under it—a couple of the men smiled and nodded.

'Thank God!' she whispered, and Clive sent her a quirk of amusement.

'You're as white as a sheet,' he told her. 'Never thought I'd ever see you as scared as you were a few seconds ago.'

'I'm not made of steel!' she retorted, just because she had to.

'No need to tell me that,' was his quiet rejoinder, 'not after last night.'

She coloured rosily and averted her head. One of the Natives began talking to Clive, much to her relief. Clive answered and the conversation went on for a short while before, turning to her, Clive said they were invited to the longhouse to meet the chief, Tua Rumah Balang.

'We shall soon have help,' he added with extreme satisfaction.

'Will it be all right to go to the longhouse?'

Clive actually laughed.

'We're among friends,' he assured her. 'There's no need for fear. Look, they're as amicable as can be.'

'They look anything but amicable,' she rejoined, but

her colour was returning as her fear subsided. Clive certainly had a way of restoring her confidence.

The longhouse—a complete village—stood on a small rise above the confluence of the two rivers and away from the swamp where could be seen masses of bulrushes and the tall spears of snow-white orchids. A long tree-trunk with deep notches in it served for a ladder and it was up this that the Natives led Faun and Clive. She smelled and saw the pigs and chickens below, as the longhouse was on piles which kept it well off the ground, allowing space beneath for the domestic animals. A verandah ran along the full length of the building and it was on this that Clive and Faun were left for a moment, the five men having gone off somewhere. But soon the *tua rumah* was standing there, having come from one of the numerous doors backing the verandah. Each 'door' was in reality the dwelling place of a family, as it was behind this that the rooms were to be found.

The verandah, Faun was soon to learn, was communal—just like the village street, in fact. All kinds of things were hanging up on the verandah walls—a lovely Ming plate of the fifteenth century, several strange brass lamps and some deer antlers. And among these, on a long pole, hung a large 'bunch' of ancient fleshless skulls, their vacant eye sockets and grinning teeth all facing outwards, towards the place where Clive and Faun were standing. She shuddered; Clive merely quirked his mouth in that most attractive way he had of giving her one of his half-smiles. That he was exultant at having fallen among friends was evident. A few dusty skulls seemed not to have any effect upon him at all.

171

'Welcome.' The word, spoken as it was in English, had the effect of making Faun jump. The *tua rumah* held out a hand which was taken first by Clive and then by Faun. The chief was a wizened man of uncertain age; he wore rather more clothing than his men, having on a sarong, and in his ears, which were longer even than those of the five men who had brought Clive and Faun here, he wore heavy brass earrings. 'You are in trouble? I hear of this, hear that you have mishap and have camp some way from here.'

'That's right.' Clive went on to explain more fully. The chief nodded from time to time. When he spoke he often lapsed into Malay and Faun became lost, not knowing what was being said. 'They're going to feed us,' Clive told her presently. 'The women are already preparing the feast.'

'Feast?' she echoed with a swift unconscious frown. 'What will it be?'

Clive admonished her with a look, and her glance flashed to the chief. Fortunately he had not understood her aversion to taking the Native food. She had better eat it, Clive whispered later in her ear. The chief would be greatly offended were his hospitality to be declined.

They were brought the food and rice wine by three women, smiling brown women with intricate tattoo patterns on their legs and thighs, with heavy brass earrings that had stretched the lobes until they actually reached the women's shoulders. Some older women appeared, dressed in sarongs, their sun-bitten faces expressionless. Fruit was produced and Clive said quietly,

'Durians; they're supposed to be delicious.'

It did seem that they were something special, the way the Native girls expressed their joy as they brought them out. But the smell instantly assailed Faun's nostrils and she stared with a hint of despair at Clive. His lips twitched, but she saw that he too was being overcome by the most obnoxious odour that came from the large ripe fruit with their long hard spines. One of the men had to chop open the tough rind, exposing seeds rather like beans, and surrounded by what Faun later could only describe as a thick slimy mass. The taste was no better. Slime, phosphorous and onions, was how Clive described it much later on. And to think, reflected Faun, that she had spent some considerable time looking out for durian trees, hoping the fruit would supplement their scanty rations! How she managed to get through the piece she had been given by one of the smiling Native girls Faun never knew. She was praying all the time that she would not disgrace herself and vomit. However, she did manage to eat and drink all that was placed before her—home-made biscuits, a few pieces of cooked pig and mouse-deer, the potent rice wine, *borak*, and another fruit that was much more palatable than the durian.

With the meal over Clive and Tua Rūmah Balang went into conference, sitting on the bamboo floor of the verandah with about a dozen or so of the men listening intently to all that was being said. Faun just stood by the wooded side of the verandah, watching the *prahus* coming and going along the river. Some were quite heavily laden with fruit and other commodities and it was clear that some trading with the coast went on. At last Clive came over to tell her that the *tua rumah* would send a Native boy out that day and soon a rescue could be expected. The boy, Anyi, was later given a note written by Clive and both he and Faun stood on the bank watching as Anyi got into his *prahu* and, with a friendly wave of the hand, they saw him sail away down the river which would take him to the coast, and civilisation.

CHAPTER TEN

IT was almost dark when eventually Clive and Faun got back to the camp. Tommy was making a meal, while Malcolm, plainly under some stress, was sitting on one of the chairs which Tommy had finished making, a cup of tea in his hand. Ingrid was nowhere to be seen.

'How did you go on?' Tommy wanted to know, straightening up from the butane stove on which a pan was standing, steam escaping from beneath the lid. 'I didn't expect you back last night, not with that storm raging.'

'We've managed to send for help——'

'What!' exclaimed Tommy, actually going into a dance of sorts. 'Tell me all about it!'

'So we're to be rescued.' Malcolm spoke quietly, just as if it were a matter of little importance to him. 'How come?'

Clive explained, while Faun turned away with the intention of going to her shelter to find some different clothes to put on. But Ingrid suddenly appeared, having come up from the aircraft. She looked with increasing disdain at Faun, her arrogant eyes deploring the unkempt appearance she made.

'So you've got back at last—and about time! Clive, I can't stand this much longer! There must be a way of getting help!' It was to be seen that the girl was coming to the end of her control. Faun frowned darkly at her, feeling like telling her that self-inflicted solitary confinement was disastrous to morale, but she desisted, feeling that she must not antagonise Clive by admonishing his girl-friend.

Girl-friend ... Was Ingrid still holding that position? Faun knew instinctively that the affair was all over and done with ... and that something was beginning, for her and Clive ...

True, he had made no mention of love, and the omission did trouble Faun. She would alternate between supreme confidence that he loved her, and uncertainty in that she had doubts about his ever marrying again. Well, time alone would tell, and this was certainly not the time for worrying about such things. Clive was terribly anxious about Malcolm; he had talked about his fears a great deal as they tramped home through the steaming jungle, and now his glance went repeatedly to the man on the chair, his head a little forward as if he had neither the strength nor the desire to hold it up.

Clive had ignored Ingrid's fractious remarks, talking to Tommy still, explaining what had happened at the longhouse.

'You should find something to occupy your time,' Faun said quietly to Ingrid. 'You could be helping Tommy with the meal.'

Ingrid let this pass, as Faun expected she would. Her eyes, filled with contempt, swept over Faun as she said,

'You look like a tramp! How you can go about in that filthy condition I don't know.' She spoke scarcely above a whisper, so that Clive should not hear her. 'Where did you two sleep last night?'

'In a cave,' answered Faun without hesitation.

'Together?' gasped Ingrid.

176

'We didn't have a cave each, if that's what you mean.'

Ingrid just stared in disgust. After a moment Faun spoke again, and Ingrid learned that help would soon be on its way.

'You managed to—to contact someone . . .?' Ingrid's mouth moved spasmodically. Plainly she was suffering from very heightened emotions. 'Why didn't you—you say so—at first——?' The next thing Faun knew the girl was clutching at her shirt, and trying her best to shake her. 'You could have told me right away! You rotten, hateful creature! Why didn't you tell me at once!'

'Ingrid!' Clive bounded towards the two girls and literally dragged the hysterical Ingrid away. 'What the hell do you think you're doing——?'

'You could have told me we were to be rescued! I hate you all! Why didn't you tell me?' she demanded of Clive while at the same time struggling furiously to disengage herself from his grasp. 'You were deliberately torturing me! You've all been against me from the start! And you——!' She looked at Clive with a sort of venomous hatred in her eyes. 'You and that thing sleeping together——!' She stopped, and Faun turned away, her cheeks flaming. Clive had brought up a hand and slapped Ingrid's face. Faun heard his voice and wondered at its control.

'If you aren't careful you'll get another. I'm having no hysterics from you, understand?'

Ingrid was sobbing uncontrollably.

'I n-never th-thought you'd ever h-hit me——'

'A necessity,' broke in Clive coldly. 'Unfortunately it

177

was the only way. I make no apologies. Faun, take her back to the aircraft!'

'I won't go with her!'

'Perhaps you'd like me to take you there myself?' Clive's face was grim and Faun shuddered. He looked ready to strangle the girl.

'No——'

'Then go with Faun!'

It was with some reluctance that Faun accompanied Ingrid to the plane. But she knew better than to disobey Clive when he was in a mood like this, for she had no desire to have his wrath brought down on her own head. She was in a way sorry for Ingrid, as she would have been sorry for anyone else whose character was so weak. Her own strength, inherited from her father, had always been so much a part of her life and actions that it had never occurred to her that it was a gift, a matter of genetics, and therefore she was one of the fortunate ones. It was not Ingrid's fault that she had lost control of her nerves, that she had become hysterical. And so Faun spoke soothingly to her when once she had her settled on the 'bed' inside the plane. Ingrid was weeping quietly now, but her mouth was twisted into an ugly line, and the venom in her eyes came through despite her tears.

'Can I bring you something to eat and drink?' offered Faun, but the girl shook her head. 'Let me get you a cigarette, then.'

'I haven't any! I thought that other box was full, but it's empty! Oh, how long will it be before we're rescued?'

'I can't say,' answered Faun. 'But the Natives we've

178

met and made friends with are going to bring us some food meanwhile. I can see if they have cigarettes——'

'You fool! How can cannibals have cigarettes!'

'They're not cannibals,' returned Faun quietly. 'If they had been then Clive and I wouldn't be here, would we?' Ingrid said nothing and Faun offered once again to bring her something to eat. 'We've brought back with us some pig meat, and some eggs,' she added. 'Also, we have some of their own kind of biscuits——'

'I don't want that foul, dirty food! You can eat it if you like, but I'm rather particular what I put in my inside!'

Faun gave a small sigh and left her. Clive was still talking to Tommy and she went to her shelter and stripped off everything. Then she put on her negligée and went over to the shower. Twenty minutes later, feeling fresh and clean—except for her hair, which was drab even though she had held it under the shower and then immersed it in the water container—she was sitting down to the meal which Tommy had prepared. Malcolm was in his bed, having been taken there by Clive. He was now eating some of the pork and biscuits which Clive had graciously accepted from Tua Rumah Balang.

'This is good,' declared Tommy, who himself had almost managed to trap a wild pig that afternoon. It had got away only because Tommy had not made the trap quite right. He had now added something to it and had high hopes of succeeding this time.

'Not bad at all.' Clive was coolly impersonal; Faun guessed that he was exceedingly embarrassed by the behaviour of Ingrid but was determined to retain his dignity as the boss of the airline. Neither Malcolm nor Tommy had made any comment on the girl's outburst, naturally, but it was obvious that they must be thinking about it.

'I feel it could be improved by a different method of cooking, though,' said Tommy, helping himself to another piece. 'I expect they're very primitive up there?'

'Not as primitive as one would expect,' answered Clive. 'They trade with the merchants of the coast, you see, taking down fruits and rice and the little mouse-deer which the Natives trap.'

'And do they get money in return?'

'I expect so, and with it they buy things like cloth for their sarongs, and we saw some very attractive rugs which I presume had been bought down at the coast.'

'Times are changing,' said Tommy thoughtfully. 'I wonder if the changes are for the better?'

'It's a matter of opinion. These tribes were a happy, contented people and I don't see why their cultures and general way of life should be changed just because some pompous would-be reformer decides to interfere.'

'They are supposed to be undernourished, though.'

'Their bodies are adapted to the food they get. They didn't seem undernourished to us.' Clive glanced at Faun, who nodded and said,

'They looked inordinately healthy, and happy. I feel they should be left alone. After all, man hasn't made such a great success of his civilised state, has he?'

'Heading to destroy himself, you mean?' Tommy made a wry gesture as he spoke. 'Too clever by far, that's man's trouble.'

Faun would very much have liked to tell Tommy

about the caves, but with the memory of one particular cave in her mind she refrained. However, she later heard Clive telling Tommy about the painting they had found, and the small objects, which Faun was asked to produce for him to see. He was excited, saying he would like to explore some of the caves.

'It's such a pity that we can't. We'll never come this way again, that's for sure.'

'If we did we'd not be allowed to explore just like that. The Sarawak government wouldn't consent to it.'

The next day two Natives arrived with food—more eggs, a small mouse-deer and, of all things, several large ripe durians. Ingrid, appearing at the door of the plane, gave a shriek and disappeared again. Faun and Clive invited the Natives to eat with them, Tommy having gone off as soon as he had risen—at about midday—to see if he had caught anything in his traps. The Natives had come quite quickly through the jungle, being used to it. But what to Faun was so miraculous was that they had found the camp without the least difficulty, merely having listened intently to Clive, who also told them about the trees being blazed along the trail.

'I asked them how long it would take Anyi to get to the coast, but these men didn't know,' Clive was telling Faun when they had departed, waving their *parangs* in the air so that Ingrid, looking through the window of the aircraft, stood petrified with fear.

'I don't suppose we can expect help for a day or two,' returned Faun. 'Will Anyi bring back a reply to your note?'

'Tua Rumah Balang said he would.' Clive looked at

181

her, an odd expression in his deep-set blue eyes. 'You've been wonderful over this,' he said, and there was a softness in his voice that sent her heart racing. 'I hate to think what it would have been like to have had two temperamental women on my hands.'

'Ingrid's not really been much trouble,' Faun pointed out.

'But no help at all.' His mouth was grim, his eyes narrowed. 'I've got to see her later,' he went on, and now there was no expression in his voice. 'I've something to tell her.'

Faun said nothing; she knew what he intended telling Ingrid—that the affair was finished. He remained silent and after a while Faun said she was going to fetch her notebook and go out searching for more flowers.

'I've to put in the orang-utan,' she added with a swift smile of recollection.

She knew she had hoped he would come with her, but she was disappointed. In fact, she was actually repulsed by his coldly unemotional attitude when, a few minutes later, she emerged from her shelter and heard him say,

'I don't want to be disturbed for the next hour or so. I'm going to my shelter to do some writing.'

'I won't disturb you, Clive.'

He swung away and a great tremor of uneasiness swept through her as she watched him disappear into his shelter. Already she had owned that his moods varied, and now she strove to find some explanation for this particular one. The intimacy of last night, following as it did the long trek through the jungle; the relief

182

they had shared on discovering that the Natives were friendly; the trek back, when on several occasions Clive had taken her hand to help her over some tangled roots or other hazards. All these had strengthened their relationship and at times Faun knew a warmth and rapture so strong that she found herself half expecting to hear from Clive's lips a proposal of marriage. But she now wondered if she had taken too much for granted. What real evidence had she that he returned her love? Very little; just a few attentions and soft words ... and the intimacy of that night in the cave.

It did seem, though, that he had begun to care ...

Faun told herself that this was not the time for him to be thinking of romance. Yet his manner towards her came as a shock that dragged her down to the very depths of despair. She felt the tears pricking her eyes as she moved away, to search for her flowers. Nature had lost its attraction, though, and she was soon in her shelter, acting in a very feminine way—weeping into her pillow.

It was much later when she emerged. Clive was just coming from the aircraft and he greeted her with a critical,

'You've been crying. What's the matter?'

'I was a little depressed, that's all.'

'Why?' he queried briefly, his deep-set blue eyes all-examining.

'Reaction, I suppose. We'll soon be gone from here.'

He frowned, puzzled by her words.

'You want to leave, surely?'

'Of course, for many reasons, but ...'

'But—what?'

'It's been—been an unusual experience.' She knew this was a lame remark, and deliberately averted her head, avoiding his cool unsmiling scrutiny.

'But not one you'd wish to prolong?' he said.

'No ... not really.' A sudden onrush of misery brought a catch to her voice. 'There—there have been such pleasant times.'

'And unpleasant too.' There seemed to be a finality in his voice that wrenched at Faun's heart. How had she come to take so much for granted! The jungle setting, the moonlit nights, the dangers, the intimacy of that night in the cave ... All these had meant so much to her; to Clive they obviously meant nothing. It had been a false situation in which they had found themselves—so far away from their own particular world, in the deep *ulu*, that primitive terrain where none but a few Natives lived.

She spoke at last, and the question came of its own volition, for she had not the slightest intention of asking it.

'Am I to work for you, Clive?'

'As a pilot, you mean?'

'Yes, of course.'

He fell silent and she began fidgeting with her fingers, her nerves all awry. She had no intention of working for him, so why had the question escaped her? It would be impossible to see him regularly, to find one day that he had another girl like Ingrid ... or perhaps a wife.

'Would you like to work for the Tarrant Line?' asked Clive at length.

She looked up, her eyes misted, although she was unaware of the fact.

'No,' she answered frankly, 'I wouldn't.'

A faint smile twisted his lips.

'Then it's just as well,' he told her softly, 'because I don't intend to allow my wife to work anywhere but—er—over the kitchen sink.'

'Clive!' She stared, a great surge of emotion preventing further speech. She was trembling, vaguely aware that he had made some joking comment about the kitchen sink, but that was not important. 'Are you—you—asking . . .' She could not go on, and with a tender smile Clive took hold of her hand and drew her towards a little shadowy recess where both he and she had previously discovered a delightful show of orchids.

'Yes, my love, I'm asking you to marry me.' His arms came out to invite her quivering body to his. She went willingly, unashamed of the tears now glistening in her eyes. She clung to him, lifting her face in silent invitation for him to take her lips. With a little triumphant laugh he accepted the invitation and for a long long while she was carried on the stream of his ardour until, heady with ecstasy and desire, she was able once more to look up into his face.

'I thought you—you hadn't fallen in love with—with me——' She broke off, to utter a self-deprecating little laugh. 'That's not very clear, but you know what I mean?'

'No,' he replied. 'It's been plain for some time that I'd fallen in love with you.'

'Just now . . .' She had no desire to think of his coldness and yet she continued, 'Before I went off to look for flowers. You weren't very nice to me, and I thought I'd made a mistake in assuming that my love was returned.'

Clive's blue eyes smiled tenderly into hers.

'I went to my shelter to do some important writing. Then I had to speak with Ingrid. I had to tell her about us; in spite of everything it wouldn't have been fair to spring our engagement on her without some warning.'

'No, of course not.' Faun began to think that he had not been quite so off-hand as she had imagined. And now it occurred to her that every sharp word he ever uttered to her would inflict the direst pain. This was love, though, and one had to endure the pain as well as the pleasure. Clive, holding her from him and subjecting her to an intense scrutiny, asked in stern and imperious tones what she was thinking about to cause that frown between her eyes. She told him, and received a little shake for her honesty.

'Do you think I would ever hurt you?' he demanded. 'No, my own precious darling, I never shall, not for as long as I live. You're all that I wanted all those years ago when I made that mistake. You are my one and only love, and never will you suffer pain at my hands.' Vibrant his voice, dark with passion were his eyes as he drew her unresisting body to his and, lifting her face, took her lips with a fierce possessiveness that left her quivering with desire.

They walked a little after that, and Clive confessed that although he himself was thoroughly ashamed of the way Ingrid was behaving, he hated to hear Faun say things about her simply because it increased his embarrassment.

'I'd never seen that side of her,' he admitted. 'She was merely a pretty plaything——' He stopped frowning heavily. 'No more of Ingrid!' he almost snapped. 'She's in the past.'

'And it's the present and the future that concerns us,' murmured Faun close to his cheek. He made no comment and with a little spurt of mischief which she could not resist she said, 'You're sure, dearest Clive, that you don't mind marrying a dead bore?'

She was shaken thoroughly, and warned that she would receive much more than that if she gave her future husband any more of her sauce. When she got her breath back she reminded him that he did say it and she was sure that at the time he really meant it.

'Well, that was then and this is now! You could never be a bore—a tantalising little wretch, maybe, but never a bore.' He was laughing at her and she responded. And he kissed her lips while they were parted, taking his fill of their sweetness.

She lay against him after a while, her eyes dark and drowsy with love. The sounds of the forest came to them in their silence—the drone of cicadas mingling with the distant soaring cry of the gibbons, the lovely call of a yellow-crowned bulbul, the murmur of a tropical breeze drifting down from the mountains ...

Have you missed any of these best-selling Harlequin Romances?

By popular demand... to help complete your collection of Harlequin Romances

48 titles listed on the following pages...

Harlequin Reissues

Harlequin Reissues

Complete and mail this coupon today!

Harlequin Reader Service
MPO Box 707
Niagara Falls, N.Y. 14302·

In Canada:
649 Ontario St.
Stratford, Ont. N5A 6W2

Please send me the following Harlequin Romances. I am enclosing my check or money order for 95¢ for each novel ordered, plus 25¢ to cover postage and handling.

☐ 1282	☐ 1394	☐ 1481
☐ 1284		☐ 1483
☐ 1285	☐ 1433	☐ 1484
☐ 1288	☐ 1435	☐ 1638
☐ 1289	☐ 1439	☐ 1643
☐ 1292	☐ 1440	☐ 1647
☐ 1293	☐ 1444	☐ 1651
☐ 1294	☐ 1449	☐ 1652
☐ 1295	☐ 1456	☐ 1654
☐ 1353	☐ 1457	☐ 1659
☐ 1363		☐ 1675
☐ 1305	☐ 1464	☐ 1677
☐ 1368	☐ 1468	☐ 1686
☐ 1371	☐ 1473	☐ 1691
☐ 1372	☐ 1475	☐ 1695
☐ 1384	☐ 1477	☐ 1697
☐ 1390	☐ 1478	

Number of novels checked _____ @ 95¢ each = $_____

N.Y. and N.J. residents add appropriate sales tax $_____

Postage and handling $____.25

                                        TOTAL $_____

NAME _____
                        (Please print)

ADDRESS _____

CITY _____

STATE/PROV. _____   ZIP/POSTAL CODE _____

ROM 2163